DOC

Steel Patriots MC

Book Two

I0545775

Mary Kennedy

CHAPTER ONE

Jack "Doc" Harris stood before the military action and disciplinary review board, his posture stiff and erect, his uniform laden with ribbons and medals from nearly fifteen years of remarkable service as an Army Ranger, medic, and now part of the elite team of spec ops members led by Eric "Ghost" Stanton.

The heat was stifling – dry heat my ass - and he felt the trickles of sweat rolling down his back, his boxers already soaked with his own perspiration. One lone fan, its blades barely hanging on, was blowing directly on the panel, but he stood sweating his ass off, bearing their scrutiny.

He eyed the table of all men as they read and reread the reports from their most recent mission. Twelve schoolgirls, all under the age of nine, were kidnapped and allegedly held for ransom. Except it had all been a ploy of the terrorists who took the children. There was no ransom. There was never an intent to return the girls, and it wasn't a kidnapping. It was a massacre. The girls were beaten, raped, and mutilated before they were left hanging on the side of a cliff.

In the eyes of the board, they'd gone against orders, cutting the girls down and returning them to their parents. That wasn't the grievance. The grievance was the team had not returned with the bodies of the girls as directed. Once found, technically, their mission was over.

Instead, Ghost and the rest of the team opted to hunt the fucking killers down. Doc was more than happy to oblige. In all his years, he'd never seen anything so awful. Those twelve innocent bodies were dangling in the wind, their unheard cries echoing in the dust of that shithole of a country.

No, he didn't regret his actions, not one damn bit. They were charged with rescuing those children and bringing the kidnappers to justice. Just because the girls were killed didn't mean the second half of the mission shouldn't be completed. They hunted those men down like the dogs they were and killed every last one of them. In Doc's mind, they'd rid the world of vermin not worth the space they occupied on this big blue marble.

Sure, you could argue that he was a medic, a master's in nursing if you wanted to be technical, that he should be saving people, not killing them. But his Ranger code took hold more often than not. Some people just weren't worth the use of the equipment.

Doc recited the Army Ranger creed in his head as the table continued to murmur amongst themselves.

*Recognizing that I volunteered as a Ranger, fully knowing the hazards of my chosen profession, I will always endeavor to uphold the prestige, honor, and high esprit de corps of my **Ranger Regiment**.*

Acknowledging the fact that a Ranger is a more elite soldier who arrives at the cutting edge of battle by land, sea, or air, I accept the fact that as a Ranger, my country expects me to move further, faster, and fight harder than any other soldier.

Never shall I fail my comrades. I will always keep myself mentally alert, physically strong, and morally straight, and I will shoulder more than my share of the task, whatever it may be, one hundred percent and then some.

Gallantly will I show the world that I am a specially selected and well-trained soldier. My courtesy to superior officers, neatness of dress, and care of equipment shall set the example for others to follow.

Energetically will I meet the enemies of my country. I shall defeat them on the field of battle, for I am better trained and will fight with all my might. Surrender is not a Ranger word. I will never leave a fallen comrade to fall into the hands of the enemy, and under no circumstances will I ever embarrass my country.

Readily will I display the intestinal fortitude required to fight on to the Ranger objective and complete the mission, though I be the lone survivor. Rangers, lead the way.

"Sgt. Harris? You were asked a question," said the man sitting on the far left of the dais. Doc knew him to be a fair commander of his men, but he also knew that this was a lynching of the twenty-first-century variety.

"I'm sorry, sir, could you repeat the question?" asked Doc.

"I asked if you felt your reasons were justified for going against the direct orders of your commander."

"I followed orders, sir. My team and I returned those children to their parents and then hunted down the kidnappers. Had we found those girls with the kidnappers, we would have rescued them, killing the kidnappers at the same time. This seemed a justified decision in my mind, sir." Doc stared straight ahead, never looking at any of the men in front of him. Each man on the team had endured the questioning, Ghost more than anyone as their team lead.

"You were ordered to bring those children back alive, and if they weren't alive, bring them home and you with them. You were not told to hunt down the kidnappers if they were gone."

"It was a decision the team chose to make in the moment, sir, and one I do not regret."

"You don't regret it?" asked General Whitman. "You don't regret hunting down six men, cutting them to pieces, and then blowing them up in an abandoned house?"

Doc slowly brought his gaze down to match the eyes that were staring up at him. At six-foot-five, Doc wasn't intimated by any man, any size. He might be a medic, but make no mistake, he'd completed his Army Ranger training and was the fucking best at what he did.

"I do not regret it, sir. And I might suggest if you'd seen those children hanging from a cliff, cut, beaten, and abused, vultures feeding on their flesh, you might have made the same decision, sir."

"But we didn't get to see that," said Whitman, "did we, son? Your team acted impulsively and without authority under the leadership of Lt. Stanton."

"Would you like to see, sir?" asked Doc with a smirk.

"What did you say?" said Admiral Crossing.

"Would you like to see, sir? Would you like to see the bodies of those children? Because I made sure there was evidence of what happened to them. Now, you can strip me of rank; you can court-martial me; you can ask me to leave, but by damned, the world will know why we did what we did."

"Show us the photos," said Admiral Crossing, glaring at the audacity of the younger man standing before him.

"I don't think..." started Whitman.

"I don't give a shit what you think, Whit. I want to see what those boys had to look at, what would make this elite team go off the rails as they did." The others on the panel nodded, and Doc stepped forward, opening his phone, swiping from one photo to the next.

Two of the men looked away, swallowing the bile rising in their throats. Another simply stood, not wanting to look any further. Crossing and Whitman grimaced as one picture after another flashed before them.

Doc closed the phone, securing it in his pocket once more. His teammates, Eric "Ghost" Stanton, Tyler "Tango" Green, Wade "Whiskey" English, Gunner "Gunner" Michaels, and Diego "Razor" Salcedo, were seated outside but could definitely hear. They'd all given their testimony, but none knew that Doc had photos of the girls.

"We'd like a few moments to discuss this new development," said Admiral Crossing. Doc nodded, standing to exit the hearing room. As he entered the hallway, they gathered together at one end, away from the prying eyes and ears of others.

"Fucking hell, Doc, we didn't know you had photos," said Ghost.

"I know. I took them when we were cutting the girls down. Don't ask me why. I know it's a violation, but I just had this feeling and shit for luck, it paid off."

"Well," said Razor, "I, for one, am fucking eternally grateful. They won't court-martial us with the fear of those photos becoming public. The liberals would be screaming about human rights, and the conservatives would say the killing of those men was justified. They don't want to have to argue that."

"This shit is getting fucking exhausting," said Ghost. "I'm so damned tired of having to follow rules created by men who don't do the damn job anymore, or for that matter ever did the job." They all nodded as the doors of the hearing room opened once again. The MP waved them inside.

Standing before the committee, the men all removed their hats and stood at attention.

"Gentlemen, you have presented us with a dilemma, and I won't lie... it's one I hate," said Admiral Crossing. "Your work as a unit has been indisputable, but we are getting pressures from the country's government claiming you murdered innocent men."

Doc and Ghost both started to speak, but the Admiral held up his hand.

"I didn't say I agree. However, we are tasked with making a show of... hell, I don't even know anymore. We are asking you to retire, gentlemen. If you refuse, you will be dishonorably discharged. If you take the retirement, there will be no mark on your records. It saddens me to do this, to lose some of the finest men I know and that I know we need in our service."

It seemed like a no-brainer, but Doc was pissed that he was being forced out because of their fear of some shithole government.

"I accept retirement," said Doc.

"I accept retirement," said Ghost. The chorus was heard down the line. The Admiral nodded at them, handing them their papers that would tell administration they were taking retirement effective immediately.

"You will be expected to be packed and on the next transport home within forty-eight hours. I wish you good luck, men. The world needs people like you. I hope you find a way to continue the good fight."

Doc nodded at the men and turned to leave with his teammates. Thirty-six hours later, they were seated on a transport discussing their futures.

"Where will you go, Ghost?" asked Whiskey. Ghost looked at the men he'd called teammates for the last decade. Each man was hand-selected for his team, partly because he knew of their skills, but mostly because he trusted them with his life and the lives of every member of the team.

"I have a proposition for all of you. I know some of you have family back home, but nobody has an old lady that I'm aware of," he said, smirking at the men on the transport.

"Well, Tango has a mule he's fond of," said Doc with a smile.

"Fuck you, Doc. At least it's a female mule," he grinned. "So, what's your point, Ghost?"

"My point is when my pops died, he left me a huge piece of land. It's nothing special, but it's got an old garage on the property where he used to repair cars, bikes, tractors, shit like that for neighbors. The house burned down years ago, but Pops made the barn into a pretty livable space."

"Sooooo, you want us all to live there?" asked Gunner.

"No, I mean, yea. Look, I ride, you all know that, and I know that most of you do too. What if... what if we formed our own club, a motorcycle club? We pick a name, make the garage something that we can all work and maybe open a bar or some shit."

The men all looked at one another nodding. It was a good idea, but not one of them knew anything about running a business or a bar.

"I'm in," said Tango, "but I know jack-shit about operating a bar. I can fix anything with a motor, and so can most of you, but a bar? I don't know, man. I know *how* to drink, just not how to mix drinks."

"Look, it doesn't have to happen right away. MCs are pretty territorial. We need to make sure we're not stepping on anyone's toes. I'm not a fan of becoming an outlaw MC. We got our taste of outlaw in that fucking shithole we just came from, and it didn't do any of us any good. I'm suggesting that between the bar and the garage, we'll have two legitimate businesses. Maybe on the side, we sort of informally help people."

"Help people? Like good Samaritans?" asked Gunner.

"Sort of, I'm thinking more like we take jobs others won't, but only the ones we want to take. We find lost kids, kidnap victims; we help the old lady being screwed over by a nasty landlord, shit like that." The men all looked at him, raising their eyebrows. "Look, I know we've spent our entire careers doing just this kind of shit, but now we get to do it on our terms. The shop needs cleaning up, and the barn will need to be made habitable – adding more electrical, plumbing – but it's huge. I've got a shit ton of money saved from all my deployments, and Pops left me a nice little chunk of change."

"And we'd be partners?" asked Whiskey.

"Yea, we'd be fucking partners. We'd be brothers, asshole," he said with a grin. "Just like we are now. We'd rely on one another and do shit our way. No red tape, no governments telling us what to do. We ride our fucking bikes when we want; we take the jobs we want; we fuck who we want, and we drink 'til we can't drink no more." The men smiled in his direction.

"I'm in," said Tango.

"Me too," said Doc.

"Why the fuck not?" said Razor.

"Fuck, you know I'm in, asshole," said Gunner.

"I guess we need a name," said Whiskey. "How about Steel Soldiers?"

"No fucking way, asshole. I'm a SEAL, not a fucking soldier," said Tango. The others laughed and nodded. They were all from different branches of the military and loved teasing each other about the superiority of their own branch, but deep down held mad respect for one another.

"Steel Patriots," said Ghost. "The steel between our legs and the fucking patriot spirit we all still carry."

"Steel Patriots," whispered Whiskey. The others nodded and smiled.

"Steel Patriots it is."

CHAPTER TWO

Aubrey Collins slowly walked the quaint main street of her new hometown, the small boutiques and cafes inviting and friendly, already filling with holiday décor, the bright lights mixed with fall colors. Passing a few locals, she smiled, and they returned the smile, but it was a 'do I know you?' smile, not a hello and welcome to our community smile.

She didn't really know anyone yet, other than her patients, but that didn't count. In her line of work, you didn't run up to someone and say, 'hi, remember me – I'm your therapist.' No, that never went over well.

To her patients, she was Dr. Aubrey Collins, but to anyone who knew her well, she was just Bree. Unfortunately, the list of individuals who truly knew her well was small to say the least. Friends didn't come easy for her, men or women, it seemed. Above and beyond her own fears of intimacy and friendship, she also stood out from the crowd.

Becoming a therapist specializing in abuse and trauma seemed almost tragically written in the stars for Bree.

By the time she was seven, her mother was on husband number three. The first two weren't terrible; they were just indifferent.

Indifferent to her presence, indifferent to her hunger, indifferent to her need to be loved. She had no clue if either man was her father; her mother never told her. It was the third one that changed her life forever... that set her on this path she was currently walking.

It started about two years into their marriage. Her mother was drinking more and more, which meant she was sleeping more and more, and that meant that Carl had more opportunities to be alone with Bree. At first, it was just things like 'sit on my lap like a good girl.' She'd felt odd initially, his hands gliding up and down her bare legs, occasionally gripping the tender flesh of her thighs, making her cry out. She felt the strange thing poking her bottom and then his hand inside his zipper while she was forced to sit still. Sometimes she would feel a wetness against her clothing and think he must have peed his pants, but adults didn't do that, did they?

When she tried to tell her mother, she was spanked for lying about her 'loving' stepfather. As she got older, refusing to sit on his lap any longer, the late-night visits into her bedroom started. His hands running up and down her sleeping... or pretend sleeping... body. The wet kissing noises on her neck. She'd tried to lock the doors, but he would only pick the lock. Eventually, he took the knob off the door completely, telling her mother that she was sneaking boys inside the room or hiding things from them, and she couldn't be trusted.

At thirteen, he started touching her increasingly large breasts, telling her if she told anyone, he would kill her mother. He would sit on the edge of her bed with one hand beneath her shirt, squeezing her breasts, and the other inside his zipper rubbing up and down. He would stare at her while tears fell silently down her cheeks, him painfully digging his fingers into the flesh of her breasts, his heavy breathing making her feel sick until he would grunt and groan, wiping something wet on her bed and leaving.

Just a few weeks shy of seventeen, an incident occurred that changed her life forever. Late one night, after her mother fell into her drunken sleep once more, Carl came into her room, pulling back the covers and forcing her legs apart. He was rougher, more intent on inflicting his will than ever before. He shoved her panties down, covering her mouth with one hand, the other fumbling with that zipper once again... that awful sound of the zipper.

Bree squirmed against his heavy body, trying to cry out, begging him to stop, but he refused. He pushed her legs apart, something hard and warm pushing against her fiery red curls. She felt a sudden spurt of liquid against her, and Carl cursed.

"You stupid little cunt!" he yelled, slapping her face. "That wasn't supposed to happen. All you had to do was lay there and be quiet. I'm trying to show you how to please a man, and you can't even let me help you."

Bree curled into a ball, sobbing into her pillow. Why was this happening? What was he doing to her? It was her fault. She let this happen.

"Don't worry, Red. I'll be back soon," he smiled, leaving her bedroom. Bree leapt from her bed, closing the door. Gathering her big duffel bag and backpack, she filled it with as many items as she could squeeze into the small spaces. Pulling out the leather wallet containing her meager savings from her secret spot, she shoved the two hundred and eleven dollars into her backpack.

Opening her bedroom window, she shimmied out onto the front lawn, looking both ways to make sure no one would see her. Taking off toward the bus stop, she made it just in time to take the line into downtown. When she reached downtown, it was nearly midnight. Bree walked the six blocks to the big bus station and bought a ticket for as far away as her money would carry her. The ticket agent eyed her suspiciously, but Bree was tall and well-developed, making her look older than her sixteen years.

It might not seem far, but Marion, Ohio to Arlington, Virginia was like going to another planet. By the time she exited the bus, it was several days later, and the stifling heat of mid-July covered her in its blanket of humidity.

She had one year left of high school, and the challenge now would be surviving until she could finish. She would turn seventeen in six weeks... six long weeks. For now, she just needed to find someplace safe and then enroll in school.

For five days, she moved from one shelter to the next until a shelter director at a women's center took pity on her. Mabel Beckstein knew that the red-headed beauty was in trouble. She'd seen enough sexual abuse in her lifetime to recognize it immediately in a woman.

"What are you running from, honey?" she asked the girl one evening after dinner. Bree shrugged her shoulders. "I won't say a word to anyone. I only want to help you. You can trust me."

"I… I can't go home," said Bree, eyeing the woman suspiciously.

"I know, baby. How old are you?" asked the kindly woman, brushing her hair back away from her face.

"Sixteen, almost seventeen. I just… I just want to finish school," she said pleadingly. She lay her head against Mabel's shoulder, and the older woman comforted her in soothing tones, telling her own story of abuse and escape as a battered wife. Bree felt more and more connected to the woman and opened up, telling her everything.

"Well, then, let's see what we can do, okay?" Mabel made call after call until she found a home willing to take Bree on only Mabel's word. They had a basement apartment which would give her a safe place to stay, and she could attend the local high school, which was in a good area of town.

Mabel did a little background work to make sure no one was looking for Bree, and no surprise, nothing had been filed. No doubt Carl was concerned she would tell the police if they found her and convinced her mother she was just a runaway. Getting her records was easier than it should have been, and in the fall, Bree was an entering senior.

It wasn't the last time Mabel helped Bree, but it was the beginning of their two-decade friendship. She'd helped her apply for scholarships to college, helped her to get two jobs so that she could live on her own, and she was there the day she'd graduated with her degree.

Bree took the last sip of coffee, the now cool beverage sliding down her throat with ease. It would have been so easy to have been a victim, but she ran, and it was the best decision of her life. She never knew what happened to Carl, or her mother for that matter, and she never went back to Ohio.

This was her new life. This town, Stone Fork, Virginia, was her new starting point, her new beginning, and she was going to make the best of it.

CHAPTER THREE

Doc Seven Years Later...

Doc watched his friend's woman as she stepped off the bike in front of the medical building. She was seeing a therapist today, but her nerves were on edge because the psychopath that attacked her after killing her twin daughters and parents was still on the loose.

Grace found herself on the doorstep of the Steel Patriots MC, beaten, broken, and abused. It was one of the worst things Doc had ever seen. Sadly, it wasn't the first time Doc had to patch up an abuse victim. Their MC, the Steel Patriots, took jobs beyond their garage, bike building, and bar. They'd just returned from rescuing several victims of human trafficking, and once again, Doc had to patch young women together.

With Grace, he used every ounce of knowledge he possessed to get her back to a healthy physical state, but he wasn't capable of the internal, mental repair. So, he'd reached out to an old friend and asked for a referral to a therapist specializing in just this sort of thing.

That referral is what had them standing outside the medical building today. The therapist who specialized in trauma and abuse victims was willing to help Grace and see her at the MC, but she wanted the first visit to be in her office. Surrounded by Ghost, Gunner, Zulu, and Doc, Grace was ready for her first visit.

"So, Grace, this doctor has been a therapist for about ten years now. She specializes in women who have endured abuse or traumatic events. I don't know her personally, but an old buddy of mine from the Army said she was top notch."

"I trust you, Doc," she said, biting her lip. "I'm just really nervous."

"I know you are, Gracie girl, but she just needs to get this big visit done, and then she'll come out to the club and see you after that. I think it has something to do with hospital policy since she's affiliated with Mountain General." Grace nodded again, and as the elevator doors opened, they stepped down the hallway to a small office.

Doc smiled at his big friend, Ghost, and the touching, caring way he managed Grace. Not exactly known for tact or empathy, it was a shock to all of them that Ghost fell so hard for the wounded bird, but fall he did.

The waiting area only had four seats, so it was good that Gunner stayed downstairs. She pressed the button by the door as indicated and watched it light up. Taking her seat, she gripped Ghost's fingers as if she were falling down a black hole.

Doc watched her, concern filling his heart for the beautiful woman. It wouldn't be unheard of for her to suddenly feel a sense of panic and leave. Doc needed for her to stay and speak to this therapist. Grace needed to rid herself of the demons haunting her and come to terms with the death of her family. Without doing that, she and Ghost would not have a future.

The door opened, and a tall curvy redhead stood smiling at them. Her skin looked like fine bone china. A hint of freckles and a slight blush were the only coloring she possessed. She wore a simple navy-blue dress with a white blouse beneath, the collar popped at her neck. The long, curvy legs were bare, her feet tucked into a pair of professional yet sexy as fuck, navy heels. Her fire-engine red hair fell to the middle of her back, her hazel eyes staring at the room of people. Her bright smile went from face to face, stopping briefly at Doc's handsome face. She nodded at the room.

"Well, I have to assume that you're Grace," she said with an outstretched hand and a bright smile. "I'm Dr. Aubrey Collins, but my friends just call me Bree."

"Hi, Bree. Yes, I'm Grace, and these are my friends, and this is my..."

"Fiancé," said Ghost. He smiled at Grace, and she blushed furiously.

"Well, it's very nice to meet you. Will you all be staying while we're in session?" she asked the three men.

"If it's okay with you, doc, we'd like to," said Doc. "I'm Doc by the way, uh, I mean Jack Harris. I think our mutual friend, Dr. Yost, reached out to you."

Bree smiled at the handsome stranger, shaking his hand. He was exceptionally tall, which Bree found refreshing. At five-feet-ten she rarely found a man that she had to look up to. But that wasn't all. No, this man was handsome, like panty-melting, heart palpitating handsome.

He had a thick head of the most delicious chocolate brown hair falling in waves atop his head. His full beard was neat, the intense gaze of his brown eyes pulling her in. Everything about this man was sending alarms to Bree's body, and she was loving it.

"Ummm, well, why don't we get started, Grace," she said, smiling down at her patient. She turned and gave a slight nod to Doc and then closed the door.

"Fuck, that woman is hot," said Zulu, letting out a long breath.

"Don't talk about my woman that way," growled Ghost.

"Seriously? Did you not just notice the smoking hot redhead that took your woman into that room?" asked Zulu. Ghost shook his head, but Doc just glared at Zulu.

"Shut up, asshole. She's a doctor and deserves some professional courtesy and treatment. She's here to help Grace, not satisfy your sex drive." Doc flipped open an old magazine and thumbed through the pages absently.

Zulu looked at his friend and grinned. He and Doc, like all the others, served together. But where Doc was more formal than most, probably shy would be the right word, Zulu was unabashedly brazen and outspoken.

Standing the same height as Doc, at six-foot-five, where Doc was lean, Zulu was bulky and muscled. Where Doc had a thick head of hair, Zulu's head was shaved.

"Just sayin', that's some fine pussy there, Doc," grinned Zulu.

"Shut the fuck up, Zulu," he growled. Ghost looked between his two friends and shook his head.

"Enough. She's here to help Grace not spread her legs for the two of you. Find your pussy somewhere else because, so help me God, if you screw this up for Gracie, I'll fucking kill you both."

Doc nodded at Ghost, and Zulu just smiled, nodding in his direction.

An hour later, the door opened, and Bree asked Ghost to join them for a few minutes. Ten minutes after that, it opened again, and Grace, Bree, and Ghost all stepped into the waiting area.

"I'll see you next Wednesday at three o'clock, Grace," she said, smiling at the smaller woman. Bree looked up at the handsome face of the man Doc. "I suppose I'll see all of you there?"

"Yep, we'll be there," said Doc, never hesitating. Bree nodded as they left. Turning, she shut her office door and took a deep breath.

"Lord help me! That man is hot!"

CHAPTER FOUR

Bree turned the heater up in her older model sedan. The car had been a gift to herself upon graduation from her PhD program, but that was ten years ago, and old Bessie was on her last legs. She trudged up the mountain road as if gasping for air toward the home Bree was renting.

It wasn't anything special, a small two-bedroom, one-bathroom cottage with a log cabin feel to it. What it lacked in space, it made up for with views for as far as the eye could see. It also had privacy, something very important to Bree.

The car suddenly started to slow as if no matter how hard she pressed on the accelerator, Bessie was telling her this was the end of the line. *Shit!* Coming to a dead stop, she placed the car in park, engaged the emergency brake and the emergency flashers. Now what?

Looking up and down the pitch-black road, she moaned. This was the part of the movie where the masked slasher appeared, ready to chase her into the woods. Calm down, calm down.

Bree remembered that Club Steel, the bar and restaurant owned by her patient, Grace's fiancé and his friends was not far up the road, and if she heard them right, they also owned a garage on the property. With any luck, they would tow her car in and give her a lift home.

Stepping from the car, shouldering her purse, she shuddered as the wind whipped her hair around her face. Dressed in blue jeans and a white button-down shirt, she had a cardigan in the backseat, but she just wanted to find help. The road was so dark, beyond black, with no streetlights this far out and very few homes. Those that were along the road tended to be set back for more privacy and were often not visible from the road.

As she trudged up the mountain road, Bree cursed herself for not grabbing her sweater. Twenty minutes later, she looked up, spotting the sign for Club Steel and Steel Garage, and smiled to herself. Finally!

The garage seemed closed, but the big red barn-like structure was lit up like a Christmas tree, lights strung along the roofline and around the door. The neon sign was a welcome sight to Bree as she reached the double doors for the bar. Opening the door, a flood of heat hit her chilled body, and she shivered. Searching the room, she spotted Grace behind the bar, but it didn't escape her that mister sex-on-a-stick was here as well.

"Hi, Grace," said Aubrey.

"Hi, Aubrey! What brings you out tonight?" Bree shrugged her shoulders and let out a long sigh.

"Please, call me Bree, and I didn't plan on coming out necessarily. My car broke down about a mile away, and I knew the garage was close. I walked, hoping that maybe I could get a tow."

"Oh, that sucks! Of course," she said, waving at Ghost. He stood, and Doc stood beside him, walking with him. Holy hell, this man makes me glad I'm a woman. Oh hell, he's coming this way; he's coming this way.

"Hi, Aubrey," said Ghost.

"Bree," she said, smiling at the man. Grace smiled at Ghost.

"Honey, Bree's car broke down about a mile down the road, and she was hoping we could tow her into the garage."

"You walked?" yelled Doc. Bree looked up at the big man, her face shading a bright pink.

"Yes, I walked," she said defiantly. "I'm capable of walking Mr...

Mr... what was your name again?" She knew. She'd memorized that

name the minute they left. Jack Harris.

"Doc, my name is Jack Harris, but they call me Doc."

"Are you a doctor?" she asked with arms folded beneath her

beautiful full breasts. It only served to emphasis their beauty as the

movement pushed them upwards, out of her white blouse.

"No. I'm not a doctor. I was a medic while serving as an Army

Ranger and a damned fine one," he ground out. "In the military they

often call medics 'doc.' The name just stuck with me." Bree wanted to

reply something smart but didn't want to offend him. She understood the

reasoning for calling him Doc, but she wasn't happy with his attitude.

"Well, either way, I walked, and I need a tow. Is that something

you can help me with?"

"You should have called," said Doc, staring down at her. "It's

dangerous for a woman to be out at night on these backroads walking.

You could have been hit, or kidnapped, or even attacked by a wild animal.

What were you thinking!?"

"Oh really!? What... what was I... You are unbelievable. I'm quite capable of taking care of myself *Jack*," she said, staring up at him.

Ghost looked over at Grace, who was grinning ear to ear for some reason. He looked back at Doc, who was now standing with his own arms folded, nearly touching the arms of Bree in front of him. Doc was easily six-foot-five, but Bree was probably five-ten without the heels, so they were a fine match.

He finally cleared his throat, interrupting the moment.

"Well, I'll send someone to pick up your car if you'll just give me your keys, Bree," said Ghost. "I can have someone take you home when you're ready, but why don't you enjoy supper on us tonight." Bree stared straight into the eyes of Doc and then turned slowly, facing Ghost.

"Thank you, Ghost, that's very kind of you," she handed him her keys and then took a seat at the bar to chat with Grace, effectively turning her back on Doc. Ghost pulled him towards the door.

"What the fuck is wrong with you? Why were you trying to antagonize that poor woman?" asked Ghost. Doc ran his hands through his hair, gritting his teeth.

"I… I don't know. It just came out. I was suddenly so angry that she walked all that way by herself alone in the dark. Fuck! Anything could have happened to her." Ghost looked at his friend and back at the pretty red-headed doctor.

"Well, just be nice. She's important to Grace. I'm going to send the twins to get the car and bring it to the garage. Maybe you could be nice and offer to take her home." Doc nodded, not saying anything but watched as she and Grace casually chatted, laughing as they did. Her beautiful red hair cascaded down her back as she tilted her head in a laugh. Her round ass cheeks perched perfectly on the bar stool.

He groaned watching her cross one long leg over the other, the fullness of her thighs stretching against the fabric of her blue jeans. She turned sideways, watching the people of the club mill about, the buttons on her white blouse gaping, giving him a perfect view of full round globes of pleasure. His eyes moved upward until they finally rested on her beautiful face. Plump red lips, a pert nose, and hazel eyes… staring straight at him.

Doc blushed slightly, having been caught in the act of staring. But what he noticed more was that the beautiful doctor, Aubrey Collins, Bree was staring back at him, and her face was on fire.

CHAPTER FIVE

"Is he always such an overbearing Neanderthal jerk? He seemed so nice at your appointment," said Bree, glaring in Doc's direction. Grace smiled at the woman as she set her burger down in front of her.

"Doc? He's actually one of the most caring, sweet men I've ever met in my life. He's just very protective and especially protective of women. Personally, I think it's kind of nice. The Steel Patriots aren't just bar owners or mechanics, they help to rescue kidnapping victims, human trafficking victims, victims of abuse, things like that. They all have hugely protective instincts."

Bree nodded at her and then looked back toward the man still staring at her. She could appreciate someone being protective, although she'd never experienced it herself.

"I guess I'm just not used to that. I've been on my own a long time, and believe me, I've never had a man care whether or not I got home okay or worry if I broke down in the middle of nowhere." Grace looked at the beautiful woman, hearing the pain dripping from her words.

"Did you not ever have anyone serious in your life, a husband or boyfriend?" asked Grace. Bree said nothing at first, and Grace realized she might be overstepping. "I'm sorry, Bree. That was uncalled for and probably inappropriate."

"No, no, actually, I'd love to talk to another woman like this. I mean, have another woman I can talk to like this in a girlfriend way. I moved here about a year ago and have a solid patient base of mostly divorcing couples and minor issues, some in my area of expertise – abuse, trauma, that sort of thing – but, honestly, there aren't a lot of places for me to meet people my own age."

"Well, I'd love to be your friend as well as your patient if you're okay with that. But back to Doc. I think he got overprotective because he likes you."

"Likes me!" squealed Bree a little too loud. "I mean, likes me? What do you mean? I'm nothing special, Grace. If you haven't noticed, the body gods didn't bless me with your leanness. I'm packing more than a few in all the wrong places." She set her burger down, staring at her plate. "And yes, I know I don't help myself, but I love food."

"And you should! Listen, Bree, you know better than anyone that loving yourself is the first step to loving your body. You're a beautiful woman, honey. I mean stunning! You have the face of an angel, and all that red hair is simply gorgeous. I would kill to have your boobs, and don't get me started on your height." Bree blushed, staring at the woman behind the bar.

"Thank you, Grace. Truly. I know I'm hard on myself, but it's awfully hard when the world says we should all look a certain way and our genetics say, 'I don't think so.' I mean, you're so petite and gorgeous. You and Ghost make a beautiful couple. Doc... Doc is tall and handsome and..."

"Sexy?" asked Grace with a smile.

"Should you be saying that about your man's best friend?" giggled Bree.

"No, probably not, but I'm not blind. He's tall, a great face, killer body, and don't think I haven't noticed his ass and legs. I mean, whew! Although," she said, smiling, leaning over the bar, "I did just find out I'm pregnant, so my hormones are probably in overdrive right now. I want to climb Ghost every time I see him."

"Oh my gosh! That's so wonderful. Congratulations! Are you feeling okay?" Bree was very happy for Grace.

"I'm nervous, scared," said Grace. "I mean, I'm forty-one, so this could be a difficult pregnancy, but I feel... I feel like maybe this is God giving me another chance at happy. You know what I mean?"

"I do, but I don't think it's 'another chance,' Grace. I think it's just a different chance. You need to remember that you had a beautiful 'happy' for eighteen years. Don't belittle that. You were lucky you had those eighteen years. Now you get a shot at another happy. I don't think there's just one for all of us. I think there are several." Bree watched as Grace absorbed her words and decided to tell her a little more about herself, maybe helping her to understand where she was coming from.

"You know, I was a runaway, a literal throwaway, honestly. My mother was a drunk, my stepfather was, well, not nice. I never thought I'd have a chance at any life, let alone one where I finished college, but here I am doing what I love. There are always opportunities for 'happy.' Sometimes, we just have to make them ourselves."

Grace nodded at the woman, smiling. She set the glass down she was cleaning and looked toward Doc, who had a miserable expression on his face.

"Maybe you should try to grab a little happy yourself," said Grace with a big grin, wiggling her eyebrows.

"I... I don't know, Grace," said Bree, shifting nervously. She needed to leave before she made a fool of herself. Grabbing her purse, she turned to stand. "It's getting pretty late, and I should probably get home."

"I'll take you," said the deep voice from behind her. She turned to see Doc standing there, his hands in his pockets, his face with a hint of pink blush on his cheeks. "I mean, if you're okay with that. I'll take you." She nodded and scooted off the barstool.

"Do you have a jacket?" he asked, eyeing the thin fabric of her shirt. If he were being honest, he was eye-fucking the shit out of her tits and the lacy white bra through that fucking white shirt.

"N-no, I left it in the car," she said, raising her hand toward him, "and before you yell at me, I know I should have grabbed it. It is colder than I thought."

"I wasn't going to yell at you, I was going to say you can wear this," he said, handing her a warm hoodie from his hands. Bree opened her mouth in shock and then took the jacket, her fingers brushing against his, a sizzle riding up her arm.

"Thank you."

"You're welcome," he said, staring at her. Grace just looked at the two acting like love-struck teenagers. "Come on, let's get you home."

CHAPTER SIX

Bree turned slightly in the seat of the big truck, its warm leather seats keeping her bottom nice and toasty. His profile was almost better than his forward-facing view. The long aquiline nose, his strong jaw, covered in a thick brown beard. The waves of dark hair leading to a wide, manly forehead. His thick brows, lashes that would make women fill with envy covering the most gorgeous chocolate eyes. He reminded her of a giraffe, big eyes with fluttering lashes, and a face anyone would fall in love with. And that was just the face.

His chest was full, muscular. She could see it through his shirt. His lean forearms were covered in tattoos. He had thick, muscular legs she could see through his jeans. It made her panties wet thinking about those thighs touching her bare skin.

"It's not polite to stare," he whispered. Bree blushed and looked forward.

"S-sorry. I didn't mean to stare. It's just I was taking in your profile. You... you're very handsome," she said, twisting her fingers together.

"Thank you, and you're very beautiful as well, Dr. Collins." She thought she heard an emphasis on the word 'doctor' but tried to ignore it. She'd most likely offended him, and that was definitely not what she intended to do.

"I didn't mean to offend you when I asked if you were a doctor. Really, I didn't. It's just that I often get underestimated because I'm a woman, and I, well, I'm ashamed to say I just lashed out when you were yelling at me about walking. I'm sorry." Doc said nothing, just nodding at the beauty next to him. He wasn't sure that anything he might say wouldn't set her off again, and he was enjoying the slow drive up the mountain to her house.

"The next driveway is mine," she said, pointing to the left.

"You're really out of the way up here," his voice filled with concern as he looked around the small cottage. No neighbors, no floodlights, nothing.

"I know, but that was kind of the appeal, to be honest with you. I left the city because I hated all the people on top of me. When I came here, even though the town is small, I knew I wanted to live further out. Plus, patients sometimes don't respect your privacy."

"Do you have someone bothering you?" he asked.

"No, no, no one is bothering me. It's just... a story for another time," she said, smiling in his direction. She definitely did not want this night to end with her horrific childhood stories. She hoped she'd get a chance to see this man again in a better setting.

Doc put the truck in park and stepped around to open her door, holding out his hand as she stepped out of the oversized vehicle. It was the first time he didn't have to help a woman get down out of the truck. Although, in fairness, the only others were Grace and any victims they were transporting. But her height afforded her the opportunity to step down easily. He smiled and waved her toward the front door.

"You don't have to follow me," she said, looking behind her.

"Humor me," he said, grinning. When they reached the door, he gently took the key from her and opened the door. He noticed that there was only one deadbolt, and it was flimsy at best. Not wanting to anger her anymore tonight, he would bring it up next time. He flipped on the light, looked casually inside, and then nodded at her.

"Thank you for this," she said, taking her key back. She started to slide the sweatshirt off her shoulders, and he shook his head.

"Keep it. Think of me when you're wearing it." He looked as though he was going to kiss her, and she stepped back, suddenly nervous.

"I really appreciate you driving me all the way home," she stuttered.

"Sure thing. I'll call you when your car is ready if you'll give me your number. I mean, trust me with your number." He pulled out his phone, handing it to her.

"Of course," she typed her name in and her personal cell phone and handed it back to him. He quickly sent her a text, 'hello it's Jack' and smiled at her.

"There. We're now connected. The twins pulled the car into the garage, but it might be a few days. Do you need a ride anywhere tomorrow?" he asked.

"No, no, thank you. It's Sunday, so all I have are some patient charts I need to update, so I'll be busy here. If it's not ready by Monday, could you let me know, so I can find a ride to the office?" she asked.

"If it's not ready, I'll come back and pick you up to take you," he said. She started to argue, but he took a step forward. Bree held her breath. Dear Lord, he was going to kiss her. Instead, she looked down to see his extended hand.

"Goodnight, Bree. Sleep well." She shook his warm hand, holding it a bit longer than she probably should have.

"Yea, yea, you too." Closing her door, she engaged the deadbolt and then watched as the most gorgeous man she'd ever laid eyes on left her driveway... with a handshake.

Shit!

CHAPTER SEVEN

"Morning, Doc," said Skull as the big man walked through the double bay doors of the garage. "You here about the pretty redhead's car?" Doc looked at him, raising an eyebrow. Skull served in the Coast Guard for twelve years before coming to the Steel Patriots. He was six-foot-five, and a muscled two-hundred-and-fifty-pound frame. He had tattoos visible everywhere. His talent with the motorcycle end of the business was unparalleled.

"How the fuck do you know who it belongs to?" he asked. Skull laughed.

"News travels fast. You should know that. Besides, the twins were all hot and bothered by the smell of her perfume in the car. Some real expensive shit they both somehow know about, and I DO NOT want to know how they know about it." Doc could only nod, looking at the blue car up on the lift.

"Is that hers?" he asked. The car was definitely past its prime. The body was rusted, the tires nearly bald, the windshield cracked, and that was only what he could see.

"That's hers. Piece of shit that it is. She needs a new alternator, fuel pump, battery, a couple of cables are frayed. Brakes are shot to shit. She could use new tires, especially up here on the mountain. Her heater is for shit, but I can fix that with a new compressor. I can do it all, just not sure what she wants to spend on that beast."

"Doesn't matter, fix it," said Doc. Skull raised a brow at him.

"Easily over a grand in repairs, Doc. Is the lady okay with that?" he asked.

"Not sure, but whatever she doesn't want to pay for, I will. Just fix it. I'll tell her... tell her it was the alternator and that it was causing the heat to not work. The brakes she won't even see. The tires, well, I'll tell her we got a deal from a vendor." Skull nodded again, smiling at his friend.

"She mean something to you, Doc?"

"No. Maybe. Just fix the fucking car, okay?" Skull nodded. "When will it be done?"

"End of the day," he smiled.

"Thanks, Skull... and Skull? Don't let her know, okay?" He grimaced as he said the words. It wasn't that he didn't want her to know what was wrong with her car, but he knew that if she found out he paid

for all the repairs, she wouldn't accept it. He just wanted to be sure she

was safe. That's all… safe. Right dickhead.

"You got it, Doc," he said, grinning at his friend.

Doc started to walk back toward his truck and pulled out his cell

phone, hitting the number she entered only as 'Bree.'

"Good morning," said the sweet voice on the other end of the

line.

"Good morning, Bree. Are you well today?" It was so formal he

wanted to kick his own ass. Why was he so fucking nervous?

"I'm good. What's the verdict on my car?" she asked.

"It's going to be fine. You needed a new alternator and some

minor things. It should cost around two-fifty is that okay?" he asked.

"Yea, I'm surprised, honestly. I figured it would be a total gut job,

and I'd either have to bite a big bullet or finally go in the hole and buy

something new."

"No, nothing so drastic," said Doc, smiling into the phone. "It

won't be ready until this evening, so I thought I'd come and pick you up, take you to work, run some errands down near the city and then pick you up on my way back. Does that work for you? Is it too early?"

"It's not too early at all. I'm usually in the office by around seven-thirty. Are you sure it's no trouble? I mean, I could call a taxi or something."

"Bree, there are only three taxis in the whole county, and believe me, they charge a fortune. No, it's no trouble at all. I'll be there in fifteen minutes." He hung up the phone only to see Ghost walking toward him.

"You headed out?" he asked.

"Yep. Gotta pick up Bree to take her to her office. Car will be ready tonight, then I'm headed to Quantico to talk to Ivan about another shipment of girls he thinks will be coming through here."

"Fuck!" said Ghost, running a hand through his hair. "Do we think it's Krevnyv?"

"Not sure, but hopefully Ivan can clue me in. You know, it might be a good idea at some point to get Bree involved with us to help with the reintegration of some of the victims." Ghost smiled up at his friend and nodded.

"And is that the only reason we would want to get Bree involved?" Doc looked at his friend and opened his mouth to speak, and then quickly shut it. Looking over at the garage and her blue clunker, he sighed and shook his head.

"No, if I'm honest, no. But it would still be a good idea," he said, smiling at Ghost.

"Let's talk about it after this shit with the Warriors is done." Doc nodded again and headed back to the truck and down the road to pick up Bree. As he pulled into her driveway, she was waiting at the window and waved at him. Stepping outside, she locked the door and walked toward Doc.

He waited at the passenger side door, helping her into the now warm seat. Her long legs were encased in black dress pants, her upper body in a beige sweater with small flowers embroidered all over it. Doc thought it was probably the least sexy outfit he'd ever seen, yet she made it look smoking hot.

"You look nice," he said, sliding behind the wheel.

"Thank you," she blushed. "My clients expect me to dress up, but believe me, my preference would be blue jeans and my favorite cowboy boots every day. Part of the reason I set up my practice way out here was the hopes of living a less stressed life."

"And are dress clothes stressful?" he asked, smiling at her.

"They can be for a woman. Sometimes, well, sometimes the world expects you to look a certain way, and I have trouble conforming." He nodded in her direction, biting his lower lip.

"I don't think you need to conform to anyone, Bree. You're perfect just the way you are." He made the statement as casually as anything he'd ever said, but his insides were on fire wanting to reach for this woman. She returned a smile to him, and they travelled in silence until he reached her office.

"I'll be back around two-thirty or three to pick you up if that's okay," he said to her.

"That's perfect, my last client is at one, so I should be able to finish up my charts and be ready. Just text me when you get here, and I'll come down," she said, smiling at him. "And Jack, thank you again for this, for everything."

"My pleasure, beautiful," he said without thinking. Doc could feel his face burning with embarrassment, but Bree only chuckled, smiling back at him. As she reached the door to her office building, she turned

and waved.

The most perfect fucking wave ever.

CHAPTER EIGHT

Ivan Pechkin was former SAS. Russian born, English raised and schooled, but trained by both the Brits and Americans. He was used on multiple occasions in the sandbox with their team and was helping them with their current issue with the Warriors and Anton Krevnyv.

Krevnyv was a Russian crime lord with his hands in drugs, guns, and human trafficking. Which is why they were having their issue with the Warriors. That would be over with soon, but for now, Ivan might have more information that could help them stop the trafficking through their territory.

The small coffee shop in Mount Vernon was pretty far removed from Quantico, but when Doc was halfway there, he got the text from Ivan to change the location. Pulling into a spot on the street, he stepped into the cool morning temperatures and rubbed his hands together. Fall in Virginia could be stunning. The colors were changing, the reds, oranges, and vibrant yellows were blowing in the breeze, hanging on for dear life to their last hope before falling.

Doc entered the coffee shop and ordered just a plain black coffee. He never could understand all the fancy, frou-frou coffee shit. Coffee was fine by itself. No milk. No sugar. No syrup. And for fuck's sake, no whipped cream. He grabbed the hot coffee and sat in a chair tucked into the far corner of the room. From his vantage point, he could see everyone coming and going.

At exactly fifteen past the hour, Ivan walked through the doors dressed in a suit and long wool coat. He looked like a senator headed into D.C., which was probably exactly what he wanted to look like. He nodded at Doc, grabbed his own coffee, and then sat next to him.

"What's up, brother?" asked Doc casually.

"You know, I'm Russian by birth, but I have to tell you, right now, I really hate Russians or at least this one."

"That bad, huh?" asked Doc.

"The meet with the Warriors is still on for the weekend. We'll end that nastiness with you guys. Whiskey warned him the other day that if he tried to run women through your territory, you'd stop it, but the asshole believes he's invincible."

"Shit! I mean, what the fuck does he think we're going to do? We made it clear this is not something we condone."

"I know," said Ivan. "Look, I think he's going to have another shipment coming from Florida through Virginia in a few weeks. They're headed north, but I don't know where. Once I have all the details, I'll let you guys know. For now, just know that he thinks it's a big joke that you're saying you're going to stop him."

"Well, the asshole won't think it's a big joke if we put a fucking bullet in his brain," said Doc in a whisper. Ivan smiled at the big man and nodded.

"You know, Doc, I think you missed your calling putting people back together. You should have just stuck to being a plain ole Ranger."

"What fun is that?" he said, grinning at the other man. "I like tearing apart the bad guys and getting to put the good guys back together again. Now that's fun!"

"Alright, my friend, I'll let you know when I have more information. In the meantime, we'll see you Sunday night at the warehouse. Anton is especially excited to not only get his payment in the form of the drugs and weapons the Warriors have, but he's practically fucking giddy at being able to kill Scar." He shook his head in disbelief and stood, shaking Doc's hand.

"We'll be there, brother. Stay safe. And Ivan? Watch your back with Anton. I know I don't need to say it, but he's a snake of the worst variety, and you know you can't trust him." Doc's concern was touching to Ivan. Not many people worried about his well-being any longer, and certainly not a former Ranger turned biker.

"Always, Doc, always." He disappeared out the front door, and Doc sat for another twenty minutes before he made his way back to his truck. The long drive back to Stone Fork allowed him to reflect not only on the things Ivan said but on his thoughts swirling around Bree.

In all his forty-four years, he'd never met a woman quite like her. He'd never had a girlfriend of any kind – none. He'd fucked plenty. Had his dick sucked by more than a few. But not one of them was someone he wanted to keep for more than an hour.

Doc's upbringing was more than a little strange, and that certainly attributed to some of his awkwardness around women he was interested in. He'd love to be able to just ask Bree out on a date... like an honest to goodness, real date, but he'd never even done that before.

He ran his hands through his hair and blew out a frustrated breath. How did shit get so confusing? His thoughts flipped between

Bree and Ivan the entire drive until he found himself outside her office building once more. She was waiting patiently on the bench outside, enjoying the cool fall temperatures while reading a paper.

"I hope I didn't interrupt your reading," he said through the open passenger side window. She smiled at him and shook her head.

"No, not at all. I was reading an article on using role-play in trying to help childhood victims of sexual assault."

"Well, that sounds like light reading," he smirked. Bree laughed and nodded.

"Yea, I guess it sounds kind of morbid, doesn't it?"

"No, not morbid, it's admirable what you do, Bree. If I'm being honest, I wish I had more training like yours to help some of the victims we come across." He focused on the road as they headed up the mountain.

"Well, if you're interested, I'd be happy to give you some books to read," she said casually.

"I'd love that. We've got some things we're handling in the club right now, but when that's done, I'd love to talk to you some more." She nodded.

"Can you tell me… will you tell me… I mean, I know some motorcycle clubs are involved in…"

"Illegal shit?" he said, smirking. Bree nodded again. "We're not like that. Everyone thinks it because we look like traditional bikers, and we have the club and all, but honestly, the garage is one of the best on the East Coast. We build bikes from scratch. We handle the paint jobs, chrome, everything. There's a wait-list for the bikes we build."

"That's amazing!" she said.

"Yep, we're proud of it. Club Steel is really just a bar with bar food, but it makes money. It's clean, no drugs, no smoking, just a great place to hang out. The other stuff – the trafficking we stop, the helping find kidnapping victims – that's just sort of left over from our service days."

"Yea, Grace was telling me about some of that. It's really amazing what you do, Jack. I'm really impressed with what you guys take on," she said, reaching out to touch his arm. He smiled at her, and long before he was ready, they were sitting in the parking lot of the garage.

"Well, I guess we're here," he said, stepping out to open her door for her. "Let's go in, and Skull should be able to get you everything you need. Skull!" He called.

"Stop your fucking yell... oh sorry... hello there," he said, grinning.

"This is Dr. Bree Collins. You have her car ready," asked Doc.

"Sure do. Everything's good to go. Total you owe is two hundred and thirty-four dollars and a whole three cents," he said with a smile.

"Are you sure about this?" she asked.

"Positive." Bree wrote the check and took her keys, turning to see Doc still standing there.

"Thank you again, Doc, for everything."

"You're welcome, Bree," he said, grinning at her. "I'm sure I'll see you around the Club. We're open every night until midnight." She nodded and walked toward her car, turning to wave once more at Doc. Skull smiled at the big man.

"Now that's an ass that would keep a man warm in winter," he said. Doc turned to glare at him, and he raised his hands, backing up into the repair center. Doc turned and watched her leave.

"Yea, it damn sure is."

CHAPTER NINE

Bree laughed at Grace as they shared another lunch together. If she were being honest, coming to the club for visits with her patient was much nicer than seeing her in the office. For one thing, the food was good, and the atmosphere was fun. For another, there were ridiculously handsome men everywhere she looked. And not just so-so handsome – they were off the charts handsome, muscled, tattooed and sexy.

This was their third official session, but they had been enjoying spending time together over lunches or dinners at the club, and Bree hoped it would continue long after Grace needed her.

"So, you're feeling healthy? No morning sickness?" asked Bree. A familiar pang hit her gut, the desire to one day have a family of her own. That was pretty difficult if you didn't have a steady boyfriend or sex or even thought about having sex. Oh hell!

"No. I've been really lucky. The only things I seem to suffer from are occasional vertigo, and the red wine smell really sends me over the edge, but other than that, I'm good," said Grace, smiling.

"Cravings?"

"Oh, sweet Jesus, yes!" laughed Grace. "I'm craving pears for some strange reason, vanilla wafer cookies, the smell of leather and, of course, Ghost." She wiggled her eyebrows at the other woman, and Bree blushed, laughing at her friend.

"The smell of leather, huh? That's an interesting one. Maybe because you're associating it with him. I'm kind of getting used to that smell as well," she said, smiling at her friend. "How are you doing with thinking about starting another family?"

"I... I don't know. For the most part, I'm excited. I mean, I have a life growing inside of me that's part of the most amazing man I've ever known."

"But..." prompted Bree.

"But I won't lie to you. I do feel some guilt. I mean, it hasn't even been six months since my family was killed, and I'm already moving on. It just doesn't feel normal," she said, tugging at her lip.

"What's normal, Grace? No one knows the answer to that. I've had clients who lost a spouse and moved on within a few weeks. Everyone feels grief differently. We're not in the Middle Ages, and there is no appropriate timeframe for grief or for moving on. You were divorced for ten years, so meeting and falling in love with Ghost is perfectly alright. The idea of you moving on with your life, without your daughters or your parents, is also perfectly normal."

"I know that in my head, and really ninety-nine percent of the time, I'm okay with that. I feel like the girls are looking down on me, smiling that they finally get a baby brother. I don't know. I know that's silly," she said, twisting her napkin.

"It's not silly," said Bree, "it's sweet, and I can't think of a nicer memory to have than that of your daughters blessing you and Ghost and that beautiful child you're carrying." Grace nodded again and smiled, feeling somewhat lighter.

"What about your reactions around men? Are those improving at all?" she asked.

"I think that's improved more than anything. It was like once I knew Kyle was gone, I wasn't afraid anymore. I didn't feel guilty for having to shoot him, but I felt guilt for taking a life if that makes sense."

"It makes perfect sense," said Bree. "You're a kind woman with high moral character. Killing anyone, even someone who did harm to you and your family, is not something you would take lightly. I think it took tremendous courage for you to do what you did, Grace."

"Thank you. You have no idea how much our talks have helped me, Bree, and it's only been three times. Although, I guess if we count the two lunches and two dinners, you should probably bill me for that time as well," laughed Grace.

"Are you kidding me?!" said Bree. "Those were *my* therapy sessions. I've loved having someone that I can talk to as well, Grace." Bree stopped and thought about what she wanted to say to Grace. She'd wanted to tell her story for weeks now but was having trouble working up to it. She'd never told anyone her story.

"You know, Grace, I was a runaway. Sixteen when I crawled out of my bedroom window because my stepfather tried to rape me." Grace covered her mouth with a gasp. "He didn't succeed, but it wasn't for lack of trying. I bought a bus ticket for as far away as I could get and never looked back. But that kind of trauma, that kind of abuse doesn't just go away. I've struggled to have a relationship with a man. A true relationship where I could trust that he wouldn't hurt me, and I've failed miserably. I've had three boyfriends I've dated for longer than four months, that finally led to sex... not that four months is my timeframe for sex... but... well, anyway. Every time the experience left me feeling empty, not whole.

"I guess I'm telling you this because I admire you, Grace. You're a remarkable woman. Talented, beautiful, kind. I'm lucky to call you friend."

"Oh, honey, I'm lucky to have you, and believe me, I admire you as well. I'm luckier that you're my friend. Speaking of," moaned Grace staring at Doc standing at the bar, "what gives with you two?" Bree let out a long sigh staring at the sexy man. If her use of batteries for her vibrator were any indication, he was the most frustrating man she'd ever encountered.

"I don't know. I mean, I like him, really, really like him. But I get the sense that he's either not interested or shy. I mean, the first night he took me home, he was so sweet and gentlemanly. He walked me to the door, waiting until I unlocked it and turned on the lights and then shook my hand. He freaking shook my hand!"

Grace winced and looked back over at Doc, who was staring at them.

"When my car was ready, he picked me up, and I gave him back his hoodie. He handed it back to me, and he said, 'I'd love it if you would keep it and wear it now and then, thinking of me.' I mean, what man says shit like that?" said Bree in a frustrated voice. "We had these great conversations and we exchanged numbers, but I haven't heard from him since. He's always polite, and I get the feeling that he likes me, but…"

"Wow, I mean, wow. Maybe he is really shy. Look, I know he likes you, and you guys have a lot in common, I mean, both of you are involved in medicine."

"Well, he's not a doctor…" said Bree, regretting the words as she spoke. Grace only smiled and nodded.

"No, no, he's not an M.D., but he is a PA, did you know that?" Bree shook her head. "He earned his master's in nursing while he was a Ranger and then became a PA. He's the guy who patches everyone up here at the club, and I've seen him do it on more than one occasion with people they're helping. He's really remarkable, and believe me, if Ghost weren't such an ass about the man seeing my vagina, I'd let him deliver my child."

Bree broke out in raucous laughter, her face flaming red at the thought of poor Doc having to do an exam on Grace with Ghost standing over his shoulder.

"Listen, I'm no love expert, obviously, but I would just say find something that the two of you have in common and start talking. If nothing else, at least plan on joining us for Thanksgiving here next week."

"Oh, I'd love to," said Bree. "I usually just do some take-out or something, but that sounds fun. What should I bring?"

"How about a dessert or two? These guys love sweets, so believe me, anything goes over big with them." Bree nodded, making a note for herself.

"Okay, sounds great. Now, back to you. Anything else you want to chat about while I'm here?"

"Yes, we need to plan a shopping trip. I need maternity clothes, and despite what my overprotective fiancé thinks, I cannot order them online and expect them to fit. Are you up for a little shopping, maybe Black Friday?"

"Oh, girl, now you're speaking my language."

CHAPTER TEN

"You ever gonna make a move on that, brother?" asked Tango, watching his friend. Doc said nothing, just continued to stare at the table where Grace and Bree were laughing. "I mean, she's smokin' fucking hot. If you don't make a move, maybe I will."

"You fucking touch her, and I'll make sure you're pissing blood for the next month," he growled. Tango lifted his hands, grinning.

"Whoa, whoa, brother. No need for all that, but you can't just sit back and stare at something that beautiful and not expect that someone isn't going to work up the nerve to touch eventually." Tango watched as Doc continued to stare at the women. He didn't attempt to hide it. He didn't try to turn away. It was as if he didn't care that Bree knew he was staring.

"Okay, asshole, what gives? Why won't you just ask her out?" asked Tango.

"I can't," said Doc.

"You can't? What do you mean you can't? You physically can't walk over there and ask her to dinner?" said Tango, raising an eyebrow. Doc looked at him as if he would come across the bar at him.

"No, I mean, I'm not good at relationships, Tango. You are. I get that. You and Ghost both had reputations with women. I mean, before Grace, he did. Hell, even the fucking twins have more dates than I do. I'm just not wired that way." Tango saw the pain on Doc's face and, for the first time, felt bad about teasing his friend.

"Explain. Brother, no judgment, just tell me what's eating at you. I know it's something. It's as plain as the fucking nose on your face you like the woman, so what's the problem?"

"Look, I was raised in a very strict religious household. My father didn't even allow my mother to have magazines in the house like *Good Housekeeping* or *Reader's Digest*, let alone *Elle* or *Vogue*. He thought the ads showing women shaving their legs or putting deodorant under their arms was provocative and would lead to evil thoughts."

"What the fuck?" said Tango, staring at Doc.

"Yea, what the fuck. Try being a teenager, hormones raging, and your father is trying to convince you that it's only the devil trying to get to you. I was fucking scared half the time and ready to explode the rest of the time. I would wake up after a wet dream, my sheets wet and sticky, and be completely humiliated, and concerned I was going to hell. My poor mother had to make sure her arms were covered; her skirts were below her knees, and that she covered her chest."

"Jesus, dude, I'm so fucking sorry. I mean, it's embarrassing for any teenager, but to feel guilty about it really sucks. I mean, hell, my mom used to ask me every morning if I had a good dream." Tango shook his head. "She thought she was being a 'cool' mom by asking me about wet dreams. I was so fucking embarrassed. I came home one day and found three *Playboy* magazines on my bed, some of the best pages dog-eared for me."

"Man," smiled Doc, "consider yourself lucky. When I went to college, I knew that I'd have to figure things out by myself. My father literally refused to have any conversations with me. His only words of advice were to not have any sex at all, that it would only lead to evil. Evil. I wonder if he knew the whole fucking planet was evil, and so was he for creating me!" Doc drew his fingers through his hair and took a breath.

"So, I go to college, and girls start noticing me. I mean, I'm a big guy, not terrible looking, so girls approached me. Thank God I was studying nursing. I had access to a lot of, well, let's just say, colorful and informative textbooks. But still, I was twenty when I had my first sexual encounter. It was awful. I fired early, all over her legs, and she was pissed."

"Oh fuck," said Tango, trying not to laugh.

"I know. I know. It's funny now, but then... I just didn't know what to do. I started watching porn, and believe me, that shit didn't help at all because then I was expecting every chick to drop to her knees and suck my cock or double over, hold her ankles, and let me fuck her ass. That thinking did not work out well for me the first few times. When I joined the Army, I actually listened more to the guys in the barracks. Overseas, well, overseas, as you well know, we get a lot of action, and hence a lot of practice."

"So, I don't get it. You've had a lot of chicks and a lot of practice, but you can't ask her out. Why?" asked Tango.

"I did get a lot of practice for sex, not for dating or asking a woman out. I've never asked a woman out – never. I've never had a real date. I've fucked plenty, but it was all pick-ups and one-night stands. I have never dated. I've never had dinner with a woman or gone to a movie. Hell, I've never had a woman in my truck other than Grace until Bree."

"No shit!" said Tango a little too loud.

"Hey, asshole, not helping," said Doc, staring back at the table.

"Look, man, she likes you. It's obvious you like her. Just be yourself, brother. You're a stand-up dude, smart, great shape, kinda good looking," said Tango, wincing. Doc laughed. "Just be you, Doc. Everything will work out after that. Having dinner with a woman is no different than having dinner with us, just less cussing, and burping, and, well, anything involving gas."

"Yea, yea, maybe when all this shit with the Warriors is over." Tango nodded.

"Or maybe before," he said, seeing Bree walk toward them.

"Hi, ummm, it's Tango, right?" she asked.

"That's right, beautiful. Tyler Green, but they call me Tango. Nice to see you again. I'll check you later, Doc," he said, leaving them to stare at one another.

"I hope I didn't chase him off. If you two were busy with something, I can come back later," said Bree.

"Oh, oh, no, he had... work or something," said Doc, fumbling with his words.

"Well, I was... I mean, I wanted to ask you... oh, geez, I'm not very good at this. You were asking about learning more on how to deal with victims of trauma and abuse, and, well, I have a conference coming up in Toronto in a few weeks. It's the week after Thanksgiving. It's on new theories and techniques to use with victims of trauma and abuse."

"That sounds fascinating... fun, I mean," he said, staring at her. "Well, maybe fun is the wrong word, but I'm sure you'll learn a lot of really great information." Doc rolled his eyes in his mind. He was fucking this up royally.

"Yea, yea, it should be fun... I mean good. Toronto is a beautiful city. I've been several times and love it. I was wondering, I mean, I know what you guys do here. Ghost and Grace told me, and, of course, you told me. So, I was wondering if you might like to come with me. I mean, I have an extra ticket for the conference and..."

"Yes!" he blurted out before she could finish. "Yes, I'd love to join you." She smiled up at him, her face burning with a furious blush.

"Okay then. I'll send you my flight information, and maybe we can be on the same flight. Until then, I'll see you on Thanksgiving." He looked at her curiously. "Oh, ummm, Grace invited me for Thanksgiving dinner. I'll see you then." He nodded again and smiled.

"Thanks for asking me, Bree. I'm glad you did." She smiled, laying one of her well-manicured hands on his shoulder.

"Me too," she said with a soft kiss to his cheek. He watched as she exited the club and turned to see Tango, Whiskey, Eagle, and Hawk all smiling at him with big thumbs up. He shook his head and gave them all one finger up.

CHAPTER ELEVEN

The shit with the Warriors was finally done. Their club was disbanded. Their stash of weapons and drugs was now in the hands of Anton Krevnyv, not exactly a better choice but a different choice. But most importantly, the Steel Patriots no longer had to worry about the antics of the assholes to their north.

By late Monday afternoon, they'd all had a chance to catch up on sleep, and Doc was seated in the club enjoying a hot cup of coffee when his phone dinged with a text message.

Hi it's me Bree. This is my flight info American #735 at 10:05 on the 27th.

He smiled at the message and began to furiously type back.

Perfect. Making my reservations now. What seat? I'd love to sit near you.

Bree smiled, reading the text message as she sipped her tea, leaning back in her desk chair.

I'm in 11A exit row, long legs, big body ☺

Doc frowned at the last part of the message. Somebody had really fucked with this beautiful woman's mind, and he was going to figure out how to fix that shit. A few minutes later, he had his seat and texted her again.

Perfect. I'm in 11B, long legs, big body, me not you. You're perfect.

She read the message and set her phone down. Shit. Did he think I was fishing for a compliment? Crap… crap…

I mean it Bree. You're perfect. What hotel?

She let out a sigh of relief and read the message again. She'd already booked two rooms at an upscale boutique hotel, originally thinking one of her old classmates would be joining her. She worried that maybe it was more than Doc wanted to pay per night.

Hotel is covered. I have two rooms already booked. Really looking forward to this.

Doc smiled down at his phone again.

Me too. Still coming Thursday?

Please be coming Thursday, he thought. I really want to see you.

I'll be there. In fact I thought I might stop at the club tonight for dinner. I mean you don't have to be there but just thought I'd tell you.

Bree cursed as she hit send. What are you thinking? It sounds so desperate... *you don't have to be there...* oh my God! He'll never want to go anywhere with you now. The sound of her phone ringing jolted her from her own self-deprecating thoughts.

"Dr. Collins speaking," she said, without looking at the screen.

"I'll be here, Bree, waiting to have dinner with you if that's okay," said the sexy baritone voice of Doc on the other end of the line. She felt the blush creep all the way to her hairline and smiled.

"I can't think of anything better to end my day than having dinner with you," she said breathlessly.

"Good, see you tonight. Drive safe." He hung up the phone and laid it face down on the table. Smiling to himself, he let his thoughts wander to the voluptuous curves of the woman who had been occupying his thoughts pretty much non-stop for the last few weeks. Just as he was ready to sport a serious hard-on, Whiskey and Ghost sat across from him.

Way to kill my boner.

"What's up?" he asked.

"Just got off the phone with Ivan," said Whiskey. "He says the shipment arrived in Miami yesterday. He thinks they're going to keep the girls there for a while, get them ready for the buyers and then ship them north. Anton is being really quiet about this one for some reason."

"Does he suspect Ivan?" asked Doc, concerned for his friend.

"We don't think so," said Ghost. "He's telling him about all the other shit they're doing, so it doesn't make sense that he would keep him away from this."

"Do we maybe think we need to use the daughter?" asked Doc.

"No, absolutely not!" said Whiskey a little too quickly. Ghost raised an eyebrow, and Doc looked at the two men. "Listen, I don't want to use her unless it's a last resort. We have no idea if she really knows what's going on or not. I just think, for now, we rely on Ivan to tell us about the shipments." Both men nodded at Whiskey, buried in their own thoughts.

"I'm supposed to go to that conference with Bree next week in Toronto. Do you need me to cancel it?" he asked, praying Ghost would say no.

"I don't think we need to do that, Doc. If you're not here, and we need medical attention, we'll ask Gunner. He has medic training, as much as the rest of us. We'll survive. No, I think this conference will be good for everyone," he said, smiling at his friend, wiggling his brows.

"Don't be a dick," said Doc through clenched teeth. "It's a professional conference. It's not, shit, I don't know what the hell I'm doing." Whiskey smiled at his friend.

"Just do you, Doc. Just do you."

CHAPTER TWELVE

"Hi, Alicia, it's nice to see you again," said Bree, opening the door to her office. The young girl sat next to the social worker, biting her nails and swinging her short legs back and forth.

"Hey."

"Alicia," said Brenda, the social worker, "we've talked about the appropriate way to speak to adults. Please address Dr. Collins in an appropriate way."

"Sorry... hi, Dr. Collins," she said, looking up at the woman.

"That was nice, Alicia," said Bree, smiling at the girl. "Come on in, and we'll get started."

"If you don't mind," said Brenda, "I'm just going to run to the grocery store and pick up some things for dinner. Alicia is my last client of the day."

"Of course," said Bree. "We'll be just fine. Won't we, Alicia?"

"Huh? Oh, yea, we'll be good," she said, waving at Brenda.

The little girl was only twelve, but she was already developed physically. She had full breasts narrowing to a small waist, curving to fuller hips. That physical development was part of why she was here. Her cousin had tried to have sex with her, and he was nineteen. He was behind lock-up now, but it didn't take away from the poor girl's apparent fear of men.

Social services removed her from her mother's care and placed her in foster care until the situation could be evaluated further.

"We'll be missing next week's session because I'll be in Toronto at a conference, but we'll make up for it the following week," smiled Bree. "So, Alicia, tell me how your week is going," said Bree casually.

"Um, okay, I guess," she said, biting down on her nail. Bree watched the girl, identifying one of her coping mechanisms.

"Just okay? Why just okay?"

"What do you mean?" asked the girl, staring at Bree.

"I mean, what would have made it better than okay?" asked Bree, smiling.

"I... I don't know. Being able to go back home to my mom. Not having people at school make fun of me. Not feeling..." She trailed off, and Bree stopped for a moment. There were several things she needed to address.

"Do you feel safe with your mom?" asked Bree.

"Of course, I do!" yelled the girl. Bree held up a hand to calm her. "Sorry, yes, of course, I do. It's the only place I do feel safe."

"I want to revisit that in a minute, but tell me about the kids at school making fun of you. What's that all about?" Bree knew better than anyone that kids could be cruel beyond measure, especially if you were different in any way at all. She'd experienced some of that in her senior year as someone who didn't have parents, and of course, the flaming red hair didn't help her situation.

"I only have like three changes of clothes. They won't let me go home and get my own things, so I'm stuck in this shit. I mean, stuff the social worker gave me. I need nicer stuff. You know, skirts and things."

"Okay, that seems a reasonable request. I'll see if Brenda can get you over to your mom's to pick up some more things."

"Thank you," she said, swinging her legs back and forth again. Interesting. Bites nails when nervous or upset. Swings legs when she's feeling happy.

"Now, tell me about feeling safe only at your mom's. Is that all the time?" asked Bree.

"I… I can't talk about this… I'm not supposed to…"

"Alicia, you know that our sessions are confidential, right? I don't tell anyone what we talk about."

"You mean, you won't tell the cops anything?" Bree raised an eyebrow at the girl and thought about how to word her response.

"Well, if I think it's going to be harmful to you or someone else, yes, I can speak with the police. But things like your feelings and other stuff we discuss in here is between us and us only. Okay?" The girl seemed to take that in and think about it for a few minutes.

"O-okay. Well, there's this older guy at school…"

"Older? Is he in eighth grade?" asked Bree. Alicia was in seventh grade, so if he were older, that's about as old as it would get.

"N-no… not exactly. He's an eighth-grade teacher." Bree tried to control her breathing, keeping her composure, simply waiting for the girl to continue. "Anyway, he invites girls to these parties and there are men… older men like his age… some are probably forty or something. He gives us beer and wine and lets us dance."

"And does this scare you?"

"No. Dancing and drinking doesn't scare me."

"Does he force you to come to these parties?" asked Bree.

"No. I mean, I don't have to go... or... I didn't have to go..."

"What do you mean, Alicia?"

"Well, see, my mom couldn't make her rent, and I needed some money to help her so... so I asked him if he could help me out. He said there was a way for me to make a lot of money for my mom. I just had to agree to go on a trip with him. That's all."

"I see, and what's his name?" She looked up, panicked.

"No! No, you said it was between me and you... that you would keep it between us!"

"Alicia, what this man is doing is illegal. I'm concerned that he's selling flesh, human trafficking, and I think he's trying to sell you to someone. You do not want to continue on this path with this man."

"You don't know! He's good to me. He treats me nice. He... he gives me things. He teaches me things. I'm going to be really successful someday!"

"Alicia..."

"No, I knew I shouldn't have told you. I knew it! I'm outta here!" She opened the door and ran for the waiting room door. Bree jumped from her seat, following the girl.

"Alicia! Alicia, wait!" She took off down the stairs, and Bree went after her taking the steps two at a time with her long legs, but it did no good. Alicia was faster. By the time she opened the door to the front of the office building, the girl was gone.

"Damn!"

CHAPTER THIRTEEN

Doc busied himself all afternoon waiting for dinner to roll around so he could see the gorgeous woman haunting his dreams. When he could no longer focus on work, he found a seat in the club and just waited.

An hour later, looking up, he saw Bree coming through the door of the club. It was earlier than dinner time, and by the look on her face, something was wrong.

"Bree? Bree, what's wrong, honey?" he asked, pulling her into his chest.

"Doc... I think... oh shit... I think I made a huge mistake!" she said, breathing heavily. Eagle was behind the bar and poured a glass of whiskey and a glass of water, setting it on the bar.

"Go get Ghost," he said to Eagle. Eagle nodded and headed to the thick steel door that separated the club from their meeting space and the private quarters.

"Honey, tell me what happened," said Doc. Ghost came through the steel doors and moved to sit next to Doc and Bree.

"I… I have this patient… a twelve-year-old girl. She was removed from her home because a cousin tried to have sex with her, and he was nineteen."

"Shit!" said Ghost.

"Yes, the boy is in lock-up, but the courts wanted to be sure the home environment was okay. Her residence of record is within this county, which is why I was treating her, but she's been moved to a foster care home in the city. When she came in today, I knew something was wrong with her."

"Why did you think that, honey?" asked Doc.

"She was nervous, really nervous, and she was biting her nails. She said she didn't have any nice clothes. They were all at her mom's house and that kids were teasing her, but she specifically mentioned skirts. Then she said that a teacher at her school had been inviting her to parties."

"A fucking teacher?" howled Ghost. Bree nodded, Doc rubbing her hands between his own big hands.

"She said that he was giving girls beer and wine, inviting them to the parties, and asking them to dance for his friends. Alicia, the patient, oh, shit, I shouldn't tell you that!"

"Honey, I think it's okay. We won't say anything," said Doc.

"Right. Right. Okay, anyway, she said he had older friends there. She described them as probably forty, which I guess to a twelve-year-old is old. She said he asked them to dance for the friends. When I started to ask questions, she said he was going to take her on a trip.

"Then she said he was giving her money. She said that her mom couldn't make rent, and he gave her the money telling her that she would make a lot of money and be successful if she stayed with him."

"Fuck!" Ghost stood and ran back toward the steel door, opening it and yelling the name 'Ace.'

"Don't worry, honey, he's getting our cyber guy so he can try and find out some things for us." Bree nodded again.

"I'm sorry, Jack, I just didn't know who else to call. Her social worker knows she's missing, but I have to be honest, she didn't seem upset by this at all! Alicia said she was scared, but I never got to the why she was scared part before she ran."

"It's okay, Bree," said Ghost. "Do you mind giving all the details to Ace? He's going to try and figure out who the teacher might be. I mean, how many male eighth-grade teachers can there be at her school?"

"Well, that's just it," she said, staring at the group. "She's in this school district that does these things called collectives. The kids move from one school to another in order to get a more diverse education and have the advantage of things like STEM, music, the arts, things like that. When I told her social worker what she said, she told me it was hopeless. That there were fifty-one eighth-grade teachers in the collective and two-thirds were male."

"Fuck!" barked Ghost. Bree jumped, and Doc reached for her, pulling her into his arms. "Sorry, Bree. I'm sorry, really." She nodded against Doc's chest and inhaled his scent.

"Honey, give Ace all the information while I speak with Ghost." Doc smiled at her and kissed her forehead. The warmth of his lips against her skin made Bree want to cry. Just that little bit of comfort was all she needed.

"Hi, Bree. I don't think we've met officially, but my name is Alex Mills, but they call me Ace. You can call me either name." He smiled at

Bree, and she nodded. "I'm in charge of cyber security here and can pretty much do anything that needs to be done on a computer. So, let's start with some basics."

Ace asked a litany of questions to Bree, and she nodded each time, giving him what answers she could. His fingers moved swiftly over the small tablet he had in his hands, and she couldn't help but be impressed at his professionalism. She was feeling better about having sought out their help. If Alicia were in trouble with a child predator or a group trafficking children, then maybe Steel could help.

"Okay, I think that's enough for now," said Ace, smiling at her. "I'll call you if I need anything else, Bree." She nodded and watched as he walked back behind the steel doors. Doc turned toward her and said something else to Ghost, and then left his side.

"Are you hungry?" asked Doc.

"Honesty, I didn't think I would be, but I'm starving now," she said sheepishly.

"Adrenaline will do that to you. It's okay, Bree, we'll figure this out. We're going to put some guys on this right away. We have more than thirty men here who we can deploy at any time. Ghost is going to send two men to try and find her trail. It will be okay." He let his hand settle at the small of her back and guided her to one of the two reserved tables for the club.

An hour later, she was fed and feeling a bit more like herself. Doc had talked casually with her, telling her about the club and how they all came together after the military. Although he asked about her childhood, she evaded the question successfully, diverting him with something else.

"Well, it's getting late," said Bree, rising. "I need to get home, but I'll see you in two days for Thanksgiving."

"If it's okay with you," said Doc, "I'll follow you home, just to make sure everything is alright." Bree started to protest and then heard Grace's words in her head. It was kind of sweet to have someone care so much about you they were willing to go out of their way like this.

"I'd like that," she said, smiling. "By the way, my car is running like a brand new vehicle. I don't know what you guys did, but I can't thank you enough." Doc smiled, nodding as he followed her out the door and up the mountain. True to his word, he watched her enter her house and waved. Once again, she was amazed at his kindness, expecting nothing in return.

Lord, let this man be for real.

CHAPTER FOURTEEN

For Bree, Thanksgiving had never been a big deal in her own home. Her mother and whatever man she had rarely took the time to cook regular meals, let alone holiday meals. She didn't really get to celebrate until she was out on her own. Now she was happy she accepted the invitation from Grace to join the MC today.

Bree took in a deep breath as she pulled into the lot of the club. Bikes and trucks filled the parking lot, the trees shedding the last of their colorful leaves, the rustle of their dead friends flying across the gravel.

Opening the trunk, she gathered the pies, placing one on top of the other and then settling the cake on top of that. Perilously balancing the day's dessert in her arms, she made her way to the door opening it with the toe of her foot.

Doc, patiently waiting and watching the front door, was the first to run toward her, taking the packages from her hands.

"Thank you," she said in a breathless voice. "I guess just put them wherever Grace wants dessert." He nodded as she followed him to the dessert table. Bree had really outdone herself, bringing an apple pie, cherry pie, pumpkin pie, a tray of turtle brownies, and a long sheet cake with the most delicious cream cheese frosting ever.

Doc took her coat and swallowed as he took in the vision before him. Bree wore a lavender sweater that gently hugged her breasts, curving around her voluptuous body. The dark wool skirt fell nearly to her ankles, but it didn't deter from the vision of her mouth-watering hips. He was aching to touch her.

"You... you look beautiful," he said quietly.

"Thank you," she blushed. "You look handsome yourself. I've only ever seen you in t-shirts or leather." She smiled at him, and he nodded.

"Yea, my wardrobe is rather lacking. I actually bought this dress shirt and two others, along with some dress pants for the conference. I didn't want you to be embarrassed to be with me." Bree looked up at him, and her heart nearly stopped.

"Embarrassed? To be with you? Jack, can I call you Jack?" she asked. He nodded again. "I will be the envy of every woman at the conference, every woman in Toronto for that matter. You're the most handsome man I've ever met in my life, and I mean that with all sincerity.

You could wear anything, and you would never embarrass me. I'm more worried that I won't be what you want. What you need, not what you need..."

He held up a finger to her lips and silenced her.

"You are the most beautiful woman in the world," he said quietly, "and the only woman I give a shit about what she thinks about my wardrobe. You are everything I want... and need." Bree nodded her head, her cheeks now on fire. Doc leaned closer, closer, almost there...

"Dinner's ready!" yelled George.

"I'm gonna fucking kill him," growled Doc. Bree laughed but laced her fingers with his as they sat at the long table.

Grace and Ghost sat at the head of the table, smiling. Other than Bree, they'd told no one about her pregnancy and planned to announce it here today. They'd even chosen a name already, and Thanksgiving was the time to announce it.

"Happy Thanksgiving, everyone," said Grace, smiling as she tapped the water glass. "I'm so glad everyone decided to join us today. Hopefully, the house will be ready for a true Christmas celebration, but until then, this will do."

"We want to thank George for doing most of the cooking," said Ghost. Loud applause thundered in the room, and pats on the back were given to George, seated in the middle of the long table. "It's definitely a time of thanks. We welcome new friends, Axe, Ice, and Bree. We welcome you to our family." Doc squeezed Bree's fingers, and she smiled up at him.

"We welcome new loves," he said, grinning at Grace. "And we welcome new members." The room looked at one another. Bree said nothing, just smiling at Grace.

"New members, you mean Axe and Ice?" asked Doc.

"No," said Ghost, "I mean Jack Tyran Stanton, my son who will be born in just a few short months."

"Holy fuck..." said Tango.

"Son-of-a-bitch, he's multiplying," said Zulu.

"You... you're pregnant..." said Eagle. "You... you're naming him..." Grace moved around the table, touching the shoulder of Doc and then standing in front of Eagle.

"You caught me that day, held me in your arms as you called for help. You may not remember, but I remember you whispering something in my ear. Do you remember what you said?" Eagle blushed but nodded, tears filling his eyes.

"I said you were going to be okay because only good men lived here, we would take care of you, and that you were too pretty to die." Throats bobbed up and down with emotion at the thought of this young man saying something so comforting in her time of need.

"That's right. You saved me, carried me into the arms of the man I would fall in love with. And you, Doc… Jack, you truly saved my life. Nursed me back to health. Will you both agree to be godfathers to our son, Jack Tyran Stanton?"

"Jesus, Grace, kill me, why don't you," said Doc, standing and hugging her to him. "Of course, I will." Bree leaned into Jack, lovingly laying her head on his shoulder, smiling at him.

"You know I will," said Eagle. "I can't wait to teach him all sorts of things." The mischievous grin on Eagle's sweet face made Grace laugh. Congratulations filled the air, and they all smiled at the couple.

"To us," said Ghost, "to our crazy-ass family, but it's ours."

"To us!"

For just a few hours, it was as if the world waited outside for them, waiting to pounce with its evil and depravity. But for now… now they would feast, they would be thankful, and they would secure their new friendships.

CHAPTER FIFTEEN

Doc picked Bree up early on Sunday morning to drive them to the airport. They chatted casually, both somewhat nervous about spending the next four days together. Parking the truck, they made their way inside the airport, checked their baggage, and then worked their way through security.

As the plane began to board, Bree's nerves kicked into high gear. She wasn't a great flyer, and to think now she was flying with this handsome man next to her to a city far away, her anxiety was getting the best of her.

"Don't like to fly," he said, grinning at her. Bree shook her head no and then nodded a contradictory yes. "It's okay, beautiful. I'm right here." He linked his fingers with hers and pulled her closer.

Doc inhaled the fragrance of her perfume, the perfume the twins seemed to know right away. The scent was some sort of expensive perfume that could only be purchased at a small boutique in New York. He'd have to find out more about it, so he could buy a bottle for her for Christmas. Right now, he was inhaling the fragrance, imprinting it on his brain.

He looked down at her now sleeping face; the mass of red hair sweeping over her shoulder lay partially on his arm. Her full lips were begging to be kissed, begging for his touch. The deep vee of her t-shirt made him want to reach down and touch her breasts, feel the soft skin between his fingers,

He groaned, squirming in his seat at the growing erection tenting his jeans. He had to get this under control before they landed. *Think about anything other than Bree. Ghost – what the shit! Whiskey – fuck! Ace – that did it. Done.*

Bree felt the plane begin its descent and opened her eyes, only to see Doc staring straight at her. She flushed, sitting upright, straightening her t-shit which was slightly askew and giving the entire plane a delicious view of her breasts.

"Was I drooling?" she asked, smiling up at him.

"Nooo, snoring yes, not drooling," he said, grinning at her.

"I don't snore!" she laughed.

"I don't know, Bree, I know snoring. I'm a man that's slept in the company of more than a dozen men at a time. Believe me, I know snoring and drooling." He grinned at her, and she huffed a cute tone of disagreement. He couldn't help himself. He leaned forward and kissed her lips sweetly, his tongue gliding along her opening, tasting her.

She reached a hand up to cup his jaw, rubbing her fingers along the fine hairs of his beard. They heard the directive to fasten their seatbelts, and both pulled back, flushed from the kiss.

"Wow," said Bree. "You do that well."

"You're not so bad yourself, beautiful. That was worth waiting for," he grinned. She nodded and wanted desperately to reach over and do it again. Instead, upon landing, they made their way to baggage claim, then through customs, and then outside to get a taxi.

It was much colder in Toronto than it had been in Virginia. Snow was falling at an alarming rate, the ground covered in white.

"So, what should we do first?" asked Bree. "I know there are some great restaurants here, shopping, the CN Tower is always cool if you're not afraid of heights." Doc couldn't help but laugh at her nervousness. The taxi was weaving its way through traffic, snow steadily falling but not seemingly slowing any vehicles.

"Why don't we get settled at the hotel and then make a decision. And for your information, Army Rangers don't get bothered by heights. It's sort of a job requirement," he laughed.

She smiled back at him, their fingers still linked together, just as they had been on the flight up. They'd yet to do anything except have a simple kiss. Well, maybe not so simple, but Bree was beginning to wonder if all that sexy lingerie she bought when shopping with Grace was going to go to waste. As they pulled into the covered archway of the hotel, the taxi driver retrieved their bags and set them on the curb.

"Thanks," said Doc, handing the man a fifty. "Keep the change." The driver nodded, a big smile in appreciation.

The lobby was a large ornate space with massive chandeliers, soft music filtering through the speakers, and a positively delicious holiday fragrance filling the air.

"Welcome to the Ascot! How can I help you?" asked the man behind the desk.

"We have two reservations," said Doc. "One for Jack Harris and one for Aubrey Collins." The man pecked away on the keyboard, looked at the screen, and then pecked away again. Bree smiled nervously at Jack and then looked around the lobby once more.

"I'm sorry," said the man, "it seems there's been an error. We have one room available, and that's all. We're completely sold out."

"That's not possible," said Bree. "I have the confirmations right here." She spouted off the numbers, and the man nodded at her.

"Yes, I see the reservations, and I'm so terribly sorry for this, but I only have one room."

"Damn," said Doc. "Well, I can try to get something at another hotel."

"I'm afraid most of the hotels are sold out, sir," said the desk agent. "We have four conferences happening right now in the city, and it's the holiday season. We're always busy here this time of year. You could probably find something further away from the city. We'll be happy to comp one of your room nights since it was our error."

"No," said Bree, "no, that doesn't make sense to go way out of town. How many beds are in the one room you have available?"

"Uhhh, it's a king, ma'am." Bree looked at Jack and smiled.

"We'll take it."

CHAPTER SIXTEEN

Doc and Bree found the room to be large with a comfortable seating area and spectacular views of Lake Erie, although it was currently blurred by the flurry of white flakes. Bree flitted around the room nervously, setting her toiletries in the bathroom, trying not to hog the counter space.

She hung her dress clothes in the closet and then turned to see Doc staring at her. He'd already taken care of his things and was just leaning against the dresser watching her. His long legs were crossed at the ankles, his hands gripping the edge of the piece of furniture. Bree felt herself blush.

"Jack, I promise there were two reservations. I didn't do this on purpose," she said, fumbling for the right words.

"I never thought you did, beautiful. I was just standing here thinking how fucking lucky I am that I get to spend the next four days in this room with you." Bree smiled and walked toward him.

"Is that so?" she grinned.

"That's so, gorgeous. Listen, Bree, I suck at dating. I haven't really done a lot of dating, not in the true sense of a date." She tilted her head, staring at him.

"What do you mean in the true sense?" she asked. Doc stood and let his hands glide through his hair. How did he say this without sounding like a man-whore?

"I mean I came from a very religious household where dating wasn't allowed. I was filled with all these archaic biblical notions around sex and relationships. I just didn't date much."

"But... but you were Special Forces. You were deployed overseas, and I've heard..." He held up his hand, stopping her before she embarrassed herself.

"I didn't say I was celibate. I'm not proud of the fact that I used women to scratch an itch, but I can assure you, I never lied to them." He reached for her hand, pulling her gently toward him. "Bree, I've never actually asked a woman on a date. Never. I know this isn't exactly a date, but I'd sure like to ask you to dinner tonight here... in this city. I'd like to talk to you for hours on end. I'd like to know about your favorite color and your favorite food. I want to bring you back and kiss you goodnight, and then I want to take you in this bed and never leave."

Bree felt her breath hitch in her chest, her face flushing with heat. Good lord, this man was asking her on an actual date and telling her what he intended to do when they got back.

"You... you're so honest and open," she said.

"I am, beautiful. I always will be. It's just who I am." He tugged her hand until she was pressed against his body. He brought one big hand to rest at the small of her back, his fingers splayed out, brushing against her ass cheeks. His other hand he brought up to cup her jaw, rubbing a rough thumb along her lips.

"I've never been very good with relationships either," whispered Bree. "Lots of reasons, for discussion later, but right now, I can't think of any reason in the world why I wouldn't want to have dinner with you, have a relationship with you... here... in this room." Doc smiled against her lips, touching them softly at first and then with more urgency.

Bree lifted her arms and casually folded them over his big shoulders. His hands slid down her sides, the big palms resting on the sides of her breasts and giving a gentle squeeze. Doc moaned against her lips, and Bree felt his instant reaction... the thick, long hard rod pressing against her.

She pushed her body harder against him, desperately needing to feel him. Doc lifted her off her feet, walking her toward the bed and gently laying them both down, his body now half on hers and half on the bed. He ground his pelvis against her hip, the feel of his cock more present than before.

"Oh, God, Jack, you feel so good," she murmured.

"Baby, there is nothing that feels better than you," he growled. Lifting her t-shirt, Doc found what he'd been dreaming about for weeks now. Bree's tits were easily double-Ds, and he loved every inch of them. The big white globes filled his large hands as he squeezed the fabric of her bra, his thumb rubbing over the erect nipple.

"Yes... more..." she moaned. Just as Doc was ready to give her exactly what she wanted, there was a knock on the door.

"Bellman, I have your luggage," said the chipper voice.

They stopped, staring at one another, and then Bree broke out in giggles. They'd been caught, and it felt very much like being a teenager.

Doc rose and adjusted his now painful cock. Bree blushed, looking at the hard outline, wondering how that was going to feel inside her body.

Doc peeked out the peephole and then opened the door as he realized they already had their luggage.

"I have your luggage, sir," said the young boy.

"We have our luggage already," he growled.

"Mr. Montblanc? Room 583?" said the boy.

"No, this is room 683." The boy blushed and looked down.

"I'm so sorry, sir, ma'am. My deepest apologies." He took off down the hallway, and Doc watched him practically running in the other direction. When he closed the door, he turned to see Bree smiling at him. They both burst into laughter until Doc pulled her from the bed.

"Come on, gorgeous. Let's find somewhere to enjoy a great meal, and what I know will be the best company in the city." She could only nod at him as she pulled on her snow boots, grabbing her heavy winter coat. Wrapping the wool scarf around her neck, she donned her gloves and followed Doc, who was similarly dressed, out of the hotel.

They walked for almost an hour in the cold before settling on a small Mediterranean restaurant on the water. The walk and the cold definitely helped Doc's hard-on. The restaurant space was warm and quaint but packed with what they could only assume were other convention attendees.

They both ordered drinks, and the waiter brought over hummus and pita bread for an appetizer. Bree smiled at him awkwardly and then looked back down at her plate as she took a bite.

"Tell me about you," he asked. "Where did you grow up? Your childhood." Bree stopped, swallowing her morsel, and looked up at him. Well, now or never.

"I was raised in Ohio for the most part, Marion. I didn't have a very good home life, Jack. I think it's why I do what I do now." Doc swallowed hard. That meant she probably suffered abuse or trauma as a child. "My mom was an alcoholic. By the time I was seven, she was on husband number three, and I'm not even sure if any of those three were my father. The third stepfather, he was the worst." A tear slid down her cheek, and he reached out, flicking it away with his large fingers.

"You don't have to tell me if you don't want to," he said, smiling at her.

"No, I want to. I want to have a relationship with you, Jack, a healthy one, and to do that, I need to tell you this." He nodded and waited. "He... he started by asking me to sit on his lap when I was around seven or eight, and he would run his hands up and down my legs. It just felt weird, creepy at first, but when he would ask me to sit, he would rub my legs, and then beneath my bottom reach into his pants, and ejaculate. Well, I didn't know that's what he was doing then, but I knew it was wrong.

"I told my mother, and she spanked me for lying," she said, letting another tear fall. "It got worse over the years as I developed. I have, well, I have large breasts, and he certainly noticed. When I refused to sit on his lap, he would come into my room at night."

"Fucking hell, where is he?" growled Doc.

"Jack, please." He nodded as she continued. "He would grab my breasts, and reach inside his zipper again, and masturbate. I cried every night, hoping my mother would come into my room. Then one night, when I was sixteen, he took it to the next level. He came in and ripped off my panties. He was going to rape me, but I was squirming so much I think it actually excited him. He ejaculated on me but didn't penetrate me."

"Fuck! I'm so sorry, honey, so fucking sorry." Doc was doing everything in his power to control what was building in his chest. She was exactly the kind of child they rescued, yet no one had rescued Bree. She'd found her way out of hell on her own and now... now, he would figure out how to put her stepfather in the ground.

"No, no, I had it better than most. I packed up, crawled out my window, and bought a bus ticket from my little nowhere town in Ohio to Arlington, Virginia. I stayed in shelters mostly until I found a women's shelter. The director really took me under her wing. She got me enrolled in high school, a safe place to live with a local family, helped me find jobs, and even helped me apply to college. I have no idea where I'd be without her."

"You're so fucking amazing, Bree," he said, reaching for her hand. "Where is your stepfather?"

"Jack, please don't do anything crazy. I never had contact with him or my mother after that. I severed all ties. I'm sure he didn't report I was missing because I would have told the police everything. My mother was probably too drunk to even know I was gone. I never went back. I have no clue if they're alive or dead." He only nodded, still holding her hand.

Their entrees were brought to the table, and they continued with light conversation, Bree telling him about her jobs in college, the failed relationships, and pathetic sexual experiences. As dessert was brought, she turned the tables.

"Fair is fair, handsome," she said, smiling. "What about you? Childhood? College? Girlfriends?"

"Well, you already know I've never technically had a girlfriend. My parents were... are probably considered religious zealots. I don't have contact with them anymore. My father thought sex or even an erection was a sign that the devil was within you."

"Oh wow, that's, um, unhealthy," she said, staring at him.

"Yea. And frustrating as shit," growled Doc. "I didn't have my first sexual experience until I was twenty, and it was disastrous. I had other experiences that improved over the years, but they were never serious relationships. I just never asked anyone out on a date, which is why I was so pathetically inept at showing my interest in you. I'm sorry about that."

"Don't be sorry," she said, smiling up at him. "I've loved getting to know you like this, taking our time. I mean, I don't want to take any more time, but…" He laughed, and she laughed, and for the first time in years, Doc's heart was light and full of hope.

"Well, after college, I joined the Army, went to Ranger school and became one of the elite. I spent almost ten years with Ghost and the team. During that time, I got my master's and became a PA. Some of the guys would make fun of me, nurse nightingale, shit like that. But it stopped the minute they got their asses shot, and I had to patch them back together," he laughed.

"I've been lucky to do what I love all these years and still satisfy my alpha male ass with the military, and now I get to fulfill both parts of my life that I love. I continue to serve with my brothers, helping with our businesses, but also rescuing women and children, helping the underdog."

"You should be really proud, Jack. You're an amazing man," she said, squeezing his hand.

"What do you say we walk back to the hotel, beautiful? Just you and me tonight. Let it happen the way it's intended." She nodded.

"Let's go, Jack. I have some things I'd like to try that I recently read about in one of Grace's romance novels." Doc stood stock still, staring at her as she blushed and then smiled. "Come on, handsome, times a wastin'."

CHAPTER SEVENTEEN

Doc was never so nervous in all his life. He was a forty-four-year-old man, who'd had his fair share of sex, but this was different. This was with a woman he cared about, a woman he could envision a future with and didn't want it to end after what he was sure would be a spectacular few days.

He waited patiently for Bree to come out of the bathroom. She'd excused herself when they returned to the room, and he removed his clothes, now sitting comfortably in his loose-fitting cotton pajama pants and a t-shirt. It was taking every bit of effort he had to control the growing erection between his legs.

After hearing about Bree's childhood, he'd desperately wanted to dig deeper into her stepfather and mother, but she seemed reluctant to give him that information. Unfortunately, it was not something he was going to let slide. He shot a quick text to Ace.

Personal favor between you and me. see if you can find information on Bree's mother and stepfather in Marion OH. piece of shit. need to know.

It took only a few minutes for Ace's quick reply.

Glad to. want in if you pay him a visit

Doc smiled to himself. He didn't even need to give details to the man for him to recognize what it most likely referred to. A few minutes later, Bree finally emerged from the bathroom. Doc stood and immediately regretted it because his once semi-hard cock was now standing at attention. She was the most beautiful fucking woman he'd ever seen.

Her hair was brushed out, the curls straighter now; the makeup was gone – just her gorgeous hazel eyes staring at him. She wore a dark purple satin gown, the spaghetti straps barely able to hold her large chest. The shiny fabric clung to her curves, and Doc followed the vision down, the hem resting mid-thigh.

"Jack? Say something, please," she whispered.

"You're the most beautiful fucking woman I've ever seen in my life, and I'm going to make you mine, Bree. Do you hear me?" He took one step forward and then stopped staring at her again.

"Yours? Jack…"

"Mine," he said again, taking another step.

"But, Jack…" she said as he moved closer.

"Mine." He pulled her into his embrace, his big hands settling at the expanse of her lower back, his eyes never leaving her own. "Mine," he whispered against her lips.

"Yours," she smiled. Yea, she could do this. Belong to this man, be his. Whatever that meant, she was willing to explore it for sure.

Doc ran his tongue along her lips, tasting her, absorbing every ounce of Aubrey Collins. His left hand glided up the back of her negligee, feeling the silky softness of the fabric only made him harder. He gripped the back of her neck and explored more, grinding his body against hers.

Bree moaned against his lips. Her body was literally on fire. The whole place was going to go up in flames soon if he didn't move it along. She felt the size of him against her body and knew she was already slick with wetness for him.

"Oh... Oh, God... Jack... please..."

"Mmmm, baby... you smell so fucking good... so... perfect. Tell me what you want, baby... tell me..." he said, trailing kisses along her neck, up to her earlobes.

"I... can't think when you're doing that... I... I want you, Jack... I want..." she never got to finish the sentence. He lifted her off her feet, walking them both to the bed. Gently laying her against the cool sheet, her nipples immediately poked up through the fabric and Doc groaned, tweaking one between his thumb and forefinger.

"Fuck, I love your chest," he moaned against the fabric. She felt the heat of his mouth and arched, wanting more. Gripping his t-shirt, she lifted it over his head and nearly had an orgasm. Doc looked great in clothes, but holy fuck, naked he was like a male model. His body was lean with muscle, not thick and heavy, more corded and defined. He was littered with tattoos that seemed to effortlessly float from one design to the next. His arms were well defined, the muscles long like everything else on this man.

"Holy hell, you're sexy," she said, blushing. He let out a deep laugh and kissed her.

"Not nearly as sexy as you, beautiful. You're so damned gorgeous, Bree. I need you, baby," he said, grinding into her hip bone.

"Then, for God's sake, take your clothes off!" He laughed, shoving down his pajama pants. His long, thick erection bounced free, and Bree couldn't help but wonder what that was going to feel like inside of her.

She wasn't a virgin, but she'd definitely never had anything quite so...
impressive. He pulled at the gown and lifted it over her head.

For a moment, Bree was feeling completely overwhelmed and
self-conscious. Her huge breasts were laid out for display, but so was her
somewhat round tummy, her thick thighs and hips, every ounce of her.

"Jesus, you're so fucking beautiful," he whimpered against her
nipple, "I love all these luscious curves, your milky white skin, fucking
smooth as silk..."

"Jack, Jack, please. I need you inside me, baby, please..." she
moaned. He looked up at her, grinning.

"Say that again." She looked questioningly at him. "Call me baby
again."

"Jack, baby, I'm begging... inside me now," she said seductively.
That was all she wrote for Doc. He pushed her knees apart, the smell of
her desire hitting his nostrils. He felt the hot drip of pre-cum on the tip of
his dick, and looked down to see her swipe it with her finger, licking the
drop from her delicate fingertip.

"Fuuuccck!" Bree smiled up at him, opening her legs wider.

Doc sucked on one nipple, and then the next, the tip of his hard cock entered the wet softness of Bree. He groaned in pain and satisfaction, willing himself not to release too soon.

"Shit! Condom?" he asked. Bree shook her head.

"I'm on the shot for hormonal reasons. I haven't been with anyone in two years. I'm clean. I'd like to feel you. I mean, if..."

"I'm clean, baby. I've never been with anyone without a condom, but that sure as fuck will end here. You're it for me, Bree. You are mine." With the word 'mine,' he drove inside her with one big thrust, and she gasped at the fullness. He was definitely bigger than anything she'd ever encountered before. He was stretching her, the sting mixed with pleasure.

"Oh... oh wow... yes... that's it..." she moaned. Doc smiled down at her, pushing a lock of red hair out of her face, he kissed her, his tongue dancing wildly with hers. That was it alright. Fuck, she felt good. She was hot and wet, her pussy grasping his dick like it had been there forever. He'd never felt this before – never.

"Fuck, baby... shit, you're so beautiful!"

"Mmm… so are you, Jack… oh that's it… holy hell, you've found it… right there, baby…" Doc smiled down at her knowing he'd found the spot that would send her over the edge, his cock thrust up and out and then slammed back in again, his hands squeezing and twisting the huge rosy red nipples.

"Bree… fuck, baby… please cum…" He didn't utter another word when she screamed out.

"Yes! Jack… yes!" She arched her body up to meet him, the huge tits shaking with every movement. Jack thrust harder and harder, the seemingly never-ending orgasm continuing to shoot hot cum inside her. Bree raked her nails down his back, and he groaned against her body.

Finally spent, he let his forehead rest against hers and then kissed her again. They were never leaving this fucking bed, ever.

"That was… wow… I mean… I've never…" stumbled Bree. Doc laughed.

"It was definitely tops in my book, baby, and it will remain there unless replaced by another one between you and me. You understand me?"

"I… I think I do. I mean, are you asking me… telling me," she smirked, "that we're monogamous?" Doc laughed, kissing her.

"If that's the word you want to use, definitely, baby. But we're more than that. You're mine, Bree. I will never have another woman beneath me – ever. I want us to be exclusive, yes, but I want more, Bree."

"More? Like how much more?" she asked quietly.

"All of it."

CHAPTER EIGHTEEN

Two more love making sessions and they were curled in one another's embrace. It might have been a king-sized bed, but they were both big people. Doc couldn't give a fuck. It forced them to sleep closely together.

Bree realized she didn't need the lingerie at all. Doc was determined that they would sleep in the nude, their slick wet bodies encased in the warmth of the comforter. The temperature dropped in the last few hours. The condensation, ice, and snow on the window was evidence of it.

She traced lazy circles on his chest following the intricate lines of artwork to a small heart on his lower left side with the number twelve in it.

"What does this mean?" she asked. He kissed her nose and looked down at the tattoo. He didn't really need it to remember why he'd left the Army, but he did need it to remember why he took the jobs he did.

"It's a long story, but it's why we all left the military and formed the Steel Patriots." He gathered himself and continued. "We were sent to rescue some little girls, young, all like eight or nine. The kidnappers had other ideas. They all died. I wanted to remember that, always." Bree didn't pry, sensing it was still raw for him all these years later.

"Yellow." He looked at her puzzled. "My favorite color. You said you wanted to know all the little things. Yellow is my favorite color, although it has to be a specific yellow for me to wear it. It doesn't always go with my red hair. Favorite food? I have to tell you, I'm not picky with food. I like food, really like it, and I'm not ashamed to say I have a healthy appetite."

"It's one of the many things I love about you, Bree," he whispered into her hair. Her heart skipped a beat at the words 'love about you,' but she dismissed it as just a saying.

"Anything with Tom Hanks in it is my favorite movie, although I'm a sucker for the classics." He looked at her, waiting. "You know, Rocky, Godfather..." He laughed.

"What about you?"

"Me? Well, I'm not sure guys have favorite colors. Mine would be pretty boring... navy, black, or olive green," he laughed. "Food? I suppose I'm like you, but man, I do love a good steak with a baked potato and all the stuff to go on it. Movie choices are a lot like yours, action, adventure, although I do enjoy the superhero movies both Marvel and DC. I also have a particular fetish for ice cream."

"Fetish?" she laughed.

"Yep, it has to be just the right kind, and I really love the chocolate and peanut butter swirl. Man, my mouth is watering for that shit now." Bree laughed, and he thought he'd never heard anything so wonderful in all his life.

"So, tell me what this conference will be like?" he asked.

"I signed us up for the same lectures," she smiled shyly. "We have the first one at ten, then lunch and another one at two. There's a function tomorrow night at one of my favorite places in the city, Casa Loma."

"Casa Loma, hill house?"

"Yes, that's right, smarty-pants," she grinned. "It has this amazing history that starts with a love story and has military and war themes infused. Now it's mostly used as a museum and private event space. It's pretty spectacular."

"Do we need to dress up? I mean, full suit and tie thing?" he asked, silently praying that it would not be formal or semi-formal.

"No, things here are fairly casual. Business casual for the meetings, and then the events are casual because it's so cold. I'm hoping Mabel will be here tomorrow, so I can introduce you to her." He nodded and kissed her temple.

"I can't wait to meet the woman that saved my girl," he murmured. Bree smiled at that, letting her thoughts wander to their lovemaking. He was truly a spectacular male specimen that made every one of her female parts hum. It was only a few minutes before she heard his soft even breathing. Smiling, she closed her eyes wrapped in the arms of the only man she'd ever spent an entire night with. Feeling his strength fill her body, his protectiveness envelop her, and his still hard cock pressed against her thigh.

CHAPTER NINETEEN

They'd both slept later than usual, not rising until after eight. Showering together didn't help to speed things along as it only led to Doc on his knees and Bree's legs wrapped around his face. She could barely breathe through that one, his beautifully well-muscled, long tongue working exotic magic on her pussy. Never in her life had a man eaten her the way he did.

Bree looked around the restaurant, hoping to spot her friend, Mabel, but no luck. It was packed with convention-goers with their badges hanging around their necks. At nine-thirty, they braved the temperatures and made their way to the convention center where they found the first lecture.

Two professors were discussing the possibilities that females abducted and abused were manifesting their desires and dreams through this violent form of sexual interaction. Bree could tell that Jack was not handling the lecture well. His hands were fisted at his sides as others took notes and asked questions, he glared at the men.

"I'm sorry, professor," said an older woman in the crowd, "are you insinuating that women who are abused, violently sexually abused, are living out some sort of sick twisted version of their sexual desires? Placing themselves in the position of getting kidnapped? Raped? Beaten?"

"We are just suggesting that the mind is quite powerful," he said with a clipped air of superiority. "Women often place themselves in situations they recognize as unsafe and yet still do it to experience the thrill of what they might encounter."

Murmurs filled the crowd, and heads turned, shaking in disagreement. The two men looked at one another nervously. Bree knew it was going to happen, she could feel it, and if she were being honest, she was kind of looking forward to it. Doc stood, all eyes turning to the towering man in the second row.

"No offense to either of you, but you have no fucking clue what you're talking about," said Doc.

"There's no need for foul language, sir," said the moderator.

"No? Why? Is my foul language not manifesting your desires to be beaten to a pulp by someone bigger and stronger than you?" The room chuckled and watched as the men shifted uncomfortably.

"Let me tell you two something. You sit behind a desk and write about shit that you have no concept what you're speaking of. I spent almost fifteen years in Special Forces rescuing men and women from sick, twisted, perverted people. I watched as parents buried twelve little girls, eight and nine years old, who had been kidnapped, raped, and brutally beaten."

One of the men started to speak, and Doc stepped closer.

"Don't you dare suggest that those children... fucking children... ever desired for any of that. I continue to help women escape abusive situations as do many of these people behind me. Not one... not one fucking woman EVER wanted to be in that situation. So don't you dare sit there and say these women put themselves in that situation for some perverse desire or need. There is a difference between the desire for bondage or the S&M lifestyle with a trusted partner... trusted... and rape and brutality. Don't confuse the two... ever again."

Doc was breathing heavily, and Bree reached out, locking her fingers with his own. He turned slowly and saw the beautiful expression of support on her face.

"Come on, baby. Let's leave." He nodded and turned to leave when a roar of applause broke in his direction. The entire audience stood and left the lecture, patting him on the back and giving him thanks for the courage to stand and speak up. Turning, he looked down at Bree.

"I'm so sorry, honey. I just couldn't sit there and take any more of that," he said.

"Sorry? Jack, that was the bravest thing I've ever seen. You were absolutely right, and I'm sorry that I put us in that lecture room. What a couple of pompous, obnoxious boobs!" Doc laughed and pulled her tightly into a hug.

"Come on, gorgeous. Let's get some lunch. I'm hungry for sushi. How about you?" he said, smiling.

"I'm in!"

There were several small restaurants on the outside of the convention center, and a few searches on their phones found them seated inside one. Doc watched as Bree perused the menu, smiling at her. Their lovemaking was off the charts epic, and if he were being honest, he wanted to take her back to the room right now and fuck her brains out.

Seated at the window, he felt the cold glass as snow continued to fall lightly outside. He looked across the street and stopped. His breath caught staring at the man getting out of the black town car. Anton fucking Krevnyv. What the hell was he doing in Toronto? He snapped a blurry photo and sent it to both Ivan and Ghost, waiting to hear their response.

"Is everything okay?" asked Bree.

"Hmm, oh, yea, just thinking about those idiots. I mean, who finds these people as speakers?" asked Doc.

"I know. It's unfortunate because I know there are some really good ones out there. Hopefully, the one this afternoon will be better. She focuses specifically on working with younger children who have been sexually abused. I've read a lot of her articles, and she seems pretty level-headed." He nodded at her as the waiter set down their sushi orders.

"Bree, I wanted to say again how much I enjoyed last night. It was literally the best night of my life, honey." Jack clasped her hand in his and smiled down at her.

"Oh, Jack, thank you. I feel the same way," she said, smiling.

"Good. Because when we get back, honey, this isn't going to end. You and me are going to be together permanently. Understand?" She stopped mid-bite and stared at him.

"Jack? How can you say something so firmly when we hardly know one another?"

"Honey, we know each other in the most important ways. First of all, we've been spending time around each other for weeks now. I know your favorite color, your favorite movies, your favorite foods; I know you can bake like nobody's business; I know you drive a car that needs to be given to some teenager so it can enjoy its last days." She laughed out loud at his assessment of Bessie. "I know you don't charge enough to your clients. And more importantly, you are the single most desirable, sexy as fuck, hot as Amarillo on a July day woman I've ever known."

She just stared at him, her face flush.

"I said it last night, Bree. You're mine, honey." She could only look into his eyes, the honesty seeping into her soul, his feelings of desire and want making her panties wet.

"Okay, okay, let's say I believe that you feel like I'm It. I'm what you want," she said tentatively, feeling flush rise up her chest. "Then...

then you're mine, Jack. No other women, no other dates, n-nothing. It's just you and me." Doc smiled at her, cocking his head.

"You still don't get it, baby. I'm telling you that this is it – you and me. We're gonna be married, Bree. Maybe not by the end of the year, but we'll damned sure be sleeping in the same bed every night, and that means I will never look at or touch another woman in a sexual way. Never."

"H-how… how… I mean, how can you be so certain?"

"Aren't you?" he asked, staring at her. "I mean, be honest with me, Bree. Can't you picture us together long-term? A house together, vacations, children?" She swallowed hard and looked up at him again.

"I… I… yes." She couldn't believe she said it. But dammit, it's how she felt. It's how she should feel, and isn't that what she tells her clients? Be honest and be open. Say what you want. "Yes, I can picture all of those things, Jack. I'm crazy about you, and it scares the shit out of me."

"Me too, baby," he said, grinning. "So let's be scared together." Bree could only nod as he turned back to his meal to finish his lunch.

By four-thirty, they were finished with the last lecture, which did turn out to be infinitely better than the first one. They did a quick change of clothes and met a few other attendees in the lobby for drinks, most of whom just wanted to talk to Jack about his little show at the morning lecture. He didn't like being in the spotlight and was finally saved by the ringing of his phone.

"Ghost? What's up, brother? Why the fuck is Krevnyv in Toronto?" he asked.

"How about 'hello, Ghost, nice to hear from you, Ghost,'" the other man joked.

"Don't be a fucking asshole," smiled Doc.

"You know, you'd think a man who finally got some from the hot redhead would be in a better mood. I mean, mind-altering sex?" he teased.

"Wait? How the fuck..."

"Bree texted Grace this morning," said Ghost, laughing on the other end of the line. "Said you were the hottest lover she'd ever had and couldn't wait to get you in bed again. Kudos, brother!"

"Shut the fuck up," he laughed. "Krevnyv?"

"Yea, that shit. Ivan thinks the girls are being run to or have already arrived in Toronto. He thinks they're moving from Miami to Toronto, and then Krevnyv is sending them to Russia."

"Fuck!" murmured Doc. "What do you need me to do?"

"Nothing, brother. We've notified the Canadian Mounted Police and other authorities. They appreciated the intel and will be watching. If you need anything at all, reach out to Ivan. He's supposed to arrive on Wednesday morning. Or you can call Captain Morgan Fitzhugh of the CMP."

"Will do, brother," said Doc. "How is Grace feeling?"

"She's good man, better than good." Doc could hear the smile on his friend's face through the phone. He was happy as fuck for him and hoped he'd be smiling like that soon as well. He knew he loved Bree, but he didn't want to scare the shit out of her and say it before it was time. "Be safe, Doc, and take care of that girl."

Doc ended the call and turned to see Bree speaking animatedly to an older woman. He stepped forward and kissed her cheek.

"Jack! Jack, this is Mabel," she said, smiling at the older woman.

"Mabel, it's a pleasure to meet you, ma'am. I owe you everything for saving this woman for me." Mabel looked up at him and back at Bree.

"Well, he is definitely worth the climb," said the older woman. Bree laughed and Doc blushed. They spoke for another hour before the buses arrived to take the attendees to Casa Loma.

A few more hours, and he'd have her in his arms naked again. Tick. Tock.

CHAPTER TWENTY

With drinks in hand, they did the complimentary tour of Casa Loma. Doc had to admit he was impressed at not only the architecture but the military displays and history of the building. Sitting in the center of Toronto, it currently didn't seem to be ideal but looking back a hundred and twenty years, he could see its importance.

On the main floor of the seven-floor castle-like home, a dance floor had been set up with a live band playing soft, big-band-style music. Indicative of the crowd, thought Doc. He noticed the two asshole professors he'd embarrassed earlier on the other side of the room. It seemed their colleagues pretty much ostracized them from the event, and before long, Doc saw them leave as quietly as they'd arrived.

The event was only serving heavy appetizers, whatever the fuck that was, but he knew it wasn't enough to fuel his body. Pulling Bree away from a small group where she seemed to be politely listening but not participating, he whispered in her ear.

"I'm hungry for real food and for you," he growled. She smiled up at him.

"Well, since you saved me from those people, what do you say I fix one of those?" His eyebrows raised, and she looked around the room. Grabbing his hand, Bree pulled him toward the long hallway. Finding the door she wanted, she gently pushed. No alarms, good.

"Where are we going?" he asked.

"Trust me," she smiled. Pulling him down the stairs and into the basement, she looked both ways. The basement now housed a small cafeteria and gift shop, but she also knew its other secret. Opening another door, it opened into a long dark tunnel.

"What the fuck is this?" he asked surprised, ducking his head before it cracked on the brick and concrete.

"It's a tunnel that led to the carriage house and stables at one time. It was used during the wars in the early part of the nineteen-hundreds. But now," she said, her breath visible as they huffed through the darkness, finally stopping, "now it's just for tourists. Really, really horny tourists." Bree ground her hips against him and unbuttoning her blouse, she let the garment gape open, revealing a fine lace black bra.

"Fucking hell," he growled, lifting one breast from the bra. He pulled on the nipple with his teeth, sucking it, biting tenderly into the flesh of her full bosom. Bree unzipped her jeans and gripped his hand, sliding it down inside.

"Baby knows what she wants," he said, smirking.

"Shut up and fuck me," she laughed. His long fingers found her wet slit, and he thrust two inside her as she gasped. Fuck, yes, this was hot! As stuffy eggheads partied upstairs, they were fucking in a tunnel. "I need you inside me."

He looked at her, wondering how they would manage that in the wet, cold tunnel. Despite the temperatures, his dick definitely rose to the occasion, but it would take them both forever to get out of and back into all the layers. But Bree had it figured. She shoved her jeans to her ankles, turning, she bent over, leaning against the cold wall of the tunnel.

"Holy fuck, I'm crazy about you," he said, unzipping his own pants. He stroked his cock twice, and using his own saliva for extra juice, he slid inside her.

"Yes!" she cried. "Faster!" Holy shit, he'd created a monster. His girl wanted to fuck in the worst kind of way.

"Oh, yea, baby... fuck, Bree! Sweet fucking pussy, baby..." Doc gripped her hips, thrusting in and out as hard as he could. "Play with your clit, baby... rub it for me." Bree reached down and felt the hard little nub above her pussy. Flicking her fingers back and forth, she trailed down and felt Jack's thick rod pounding into her. She brought her hand back up and furiously rubbed her clit, desperately needing to cum.

"Oh... yes... I'm gonna cum, Jack... Jack... more..." He could feel the bundle of nerves tightening around him, her juices thick and heavenly soaking his cock with each thrust. Bree released a soft cry as he felt her tense around his cock. Almost immediately, he released as well, his hot cum spilling down her legs, too much for her pussy to handle. Their heavy, white clouds of breath filled the air as their bodies began the recovery process.

Doc stood her up straight, pulling her jeans up to cover her cold ass. He kissed her, squeezing a breast in his big hand.

"You're so fucking hot, baby. You are so damned sexy," he whispered against her lips. She nodded, kissing him again and buttoning her blouse, pulling her jeans together and then her jacket.

"That was the hottest thing I've ever experienced," she said, suddenly feeling shy.

"Really?" he asked. She nodded, looking at him sideways. "Better than mind-altering sex?" She covered her mouth with her hand, stifling the gasp. Doc laughed.

"Grace," she muttered under her breath. "Oh shit, I'm sorry, Jack."

"Bree? Don't be sorry, baby. I love that you're talking about us together. I could give a shit if the others get jealous because I'm a god in bed." She swiped at his chest and smiled. "Seriously, baby, it's all good. And that was the hottest fucking thing I've ever done." He pulled her fingers toward his mouth, tasting her juices on her fingers and moaned.

"Come on," she said, pulling him toward the carriage house, "let's explore the rest." Bree led him further into the more than eight hundred feet of tunnel. They whispered sweet things to one another, stopping every few minutes to kiss, hungry once again for one another.

"Did you hear that?" asked Doc. Bree stopped, listening. It was barely there, a soft murmur, but she heard it. She nodded, and he pressed his fingers to his lips, pushing her behind him. They stepped carefully further into the tunnel, almost tripping over the offending noisemaker. It was a child, a girl.

Doc pulled out his phone. Hitting the flashlight, he saw the battered, broken, and nearly naked body of a young girl.

"Oh my God!" gasped Bree.

"Honey, run back to the house. Tell them to call the police and an ambulance."

"She's... she's my patient. That's Alicia." Doc looked down at the girl and back up at Bree.

"Go, honey, get her some help." Bree took off running. Luckily, she was in low-heeled boots. Racing toward the basement, she started up the steps when a security guard stopped her.

"Hey, you're not supposed to be..."

"A girl... a girl in the tunnel... she's beaten... call... call," she said breathlessly. The security guard immediately called for police and rescue, following Bree back down the tunnel.

"My boyfriend is with her. He's a medic." The man nodded as he spotted the phone in flashlight mode, leaning against the wall. Doc was hovering over the girl, checking her injuries.

"It's okay, sweet girl," he murmured, "I'm here to help you. It's all good. I just want to check out your injuries." Her body had only a tattered t-shirt and jeans, no socks or shoes. Doc had removed his coat and laid it over her frozen, bloody body. From what he could see, her jaw was broken, she most likely had bruised kidneys and liver; her thighs were bruised, indicating she'd probably been raped; her hands were a mess, broken nails, fingers, bones in her hand crushed. And that was what he could see.

"It's okay, honey. I'm Doc. I got you. You're Alicia, right?" She murmured something unintelligible, and Doc just kept speaking. "Can you tell me who did this, honey?"

"Men... losh of men..." she slurred. Doc heard the loud thundering steps of police officers and paramedics behind him, flashlights blinding his vision as they ran toward them. As he knelt beside the girl, he reeled off everything he'd looked at and observed.

The paramedics started an IV and lifted her carefully on the gurney, wrapping her frozen body in warm blankets. Just as they were about to move her, her small body jerked with a seizure, blood pouring from her mouth.

"Fuck!" yelled a paramedic. "She's crashing... internal damage..." Doc jumped in, helping the young man, turning Alicia on her side so she wouldn't choke on her tongue. The blood gushed forward. The young paramedic injected something into her IV, and she settled, but moments later, the line on the heart rate monitor slowed to an eerily slow beep... then to nothing."

"Oh God," murmured Bree. Doc turned to see her white face, the police officer next to her, his arm around her shoulder, gently comforting her.

"I'm sorry," said the paramedic. "She was so bad..."

"I know, man," said Doc. "You did all you could." The police asked if Doc and Bree would accompany them with the girl to the hospital. They would need to make arrangements to ship the girl home, but they also needed to get their statements.

As they waited for the final word from the doctor, the paramedic walked out and shook Doc's hand.

"You were pretty incredible in there," he said with a painful grin. "Iraq?"

"And other places," said Doc. The young man nodded, thanking him again and just walked away. Bree lay her head on his shoulder and cried softly.

"I called social services. They're going to notify her mother. Jack, who would... who would do such a thing?" she asked.

"I don't know, baby, but the Steel Patriots are going to find out."

CHAPTER TWENTY-ONE

"Tango went with social services to notify the mother. It was the worst fucking thing on the planet to watch a parent crumble, knowing they outlived their child," said Ghost.

"The Steel Patriots are going to foot the bill to bring the body home. CMP said there was nothing in her pockets – no notes, bus tickets, plane tickets, nothing. There is no passport in her name, so obviously, the Canadians are trying to figure how the fuck she got across the border without a passport or driver's license. Emergency room doctor said she'd been repeatedly raped, maybe for days. I gave him the timeline of when she ran from Bree's office. She had bruises on her inner thighs, her buttocks, back, and bruising around her mouth. They think... they think her jaw was broken because she was forced to have oral sex."

"Jesus," whispered Doc. Bree was taking a hot shower, trying to warm her body, rid it of the visions filling her brain. Doc knew it would take a lot more than a shower to kill and cleanse that shit from your mind, but he would make sure he was here to help her.

"Yea, it makes the appearance of Krevnyv all the more mysterious. I'm sending Whiskey, Eagle, Hawk, and Zulu up that way to help Ivan."

"Has he heard anything further?" asked Doc.

"Not yet. He knows something is wrong because Krevnyv has been running around his penthouse screaming at everyone all day."

"Do we think the teacher was feeding girls to Krevnyv?" asked Doc.

"Probably. Ace has it narrowed down to possibly four men. The others were all much older than what Alicia described or had families and lived in apartments. These four are all single, early to mid-forties, own their own homes, and from what we can get from the students, the girls all think they're 'hot.' Ace will be able to figure this out." Ghost sounded tired, and Doc knew he was fucking tired.

The door to the bathroom opened to a billowing cloud of steam, and Bree stepped out, wrapped in a hotel robe, smiling sweetly at him. He nodded to her.

"Let us know if there's anything we can do at this end," he told Ghost.

"Get some sleep, brother, and hug your woman." Ghost hung up, and Doc turned, looking at Grace's sleepy form lying on the stark white sheets nearly the same color as her skin; he pulled her tighter to his body and shed a tear for another lost girl.

"Everything okay?" asked Bree.

"As okay as it can be, honey," said Doc. "Come here, baby." He pulled her toward him, lifting the covers. She slid between the sheets and curled into his chest. Her hand lay flat against his chest, her red nails looking so delicate lying there.

"Who would do something so awful, Jack?" she asked innocently.

"I don't know, honey, but I know that we're going to try and track him down."

"Do you… do you think her teacher did this?" Doc said nothing, not wanting to add to the burden already filling her heart. He simply kissed her temple and closed his eyes. He didn't need to make love to her tonight. She was in his arms, safe and warm, and that was enough for now.

CHAPTER TWENTY-TWO

Bree rolled over to find a cold, empty spot next to her on the bed. It was daylight, and the snow was no longer falling, so that at least was a decent start to their day. She pulled on the hotel robe and padded into the separate seating area where Doc was speaking to someone on the phone.

"Just tell us what you need, and we'll do it, Ghost," said Doc. Bree smiled at him, kissing his forehead as she sat on the sofa. She noticed Doc made coffee in the small mini-bar area and poured herself a cup, refreshing his.

"Alright, brother, keep us informed." Doc ended the call and pulled Bree closer to his body, kissing her sweetly. "Good morning, baby."

"Good morning," she said with a touch of sadness to her voice. "What's going on? Do we need to leave?"

"No. CMP and the FBI are working this case together now. The girls that are missing are all Americans, or so we think, and of course, Alicia was American, so the feds are involved. We, the MC, will help if they ask, but it's out of our jurisdiction at this point." Bree nodded once more, snuggling further into his arms. "We should show up for the conference as planned, honey. Just in case anyone is watching."

"Okay, I just need to get dressed. There are lectures this morning and then a group outing to Niagara Falls this afternoon."

"When it's this cold?" he asked.

"Yea, it's really quite beautiful this time of year. Part of the falls are frozen, and it's just spectacular. It might be nice to just relax for the afternoon," she said with a pleading look.

"Of course, baby, we'll do the trip." After the two morning lectures, Bree and Doc wrapped themselves in the warm layers of their winter gear and then stopped in the lobby café for a sandwich before leaving. The notification of a text message alerted him to what he was waiting for. "I'll be right back, baby."

Bree watched as he stood and walked to the front of the hotel, stepping outside. She couldn't see which direction he went, or if he was speaking to anyone, just that he was outside. She took the last bite of her sandwich and tossed the trash. Standing, she moved toward the lobby just as Doc came back inside.

"Everything okay?" she asked.

"Perfect, honey," said Doc. "I was just having a word with Whiskey and Zulu. Ghost sent them up to lend a hand, along with Eagle and Hawk, who are escorting Alicia home."

"That's really so wonderful of all of you, Jack," she said, gripping his hand. "I never met Alicia's mother, but I suspect despite the circumstances, she was a good mom."

"I'm sure she was, honey." He gripped her fingers, kissing the backs of them, squeezing a little tighter as they followed the crowds to the waiting buses. Bree looked around to see if she could find Mabel but didn't see her on their bus. There were two others, so perhaps she was on one of those.

Doc could tell that Bree was nervous, her mind racing in a million directions, wondering if she could have done something different with Alicia. He needed to make her understand that nothing would have swayed the girl from doing what she thought she needed to do.

"Will you tell me about your life after you got to Virginia?" he asked. She lifted her head from his shoulder, smiling, and nodded.

"It was sheer luck that I found Mabel and the women's shelter. I was down to my last few dollars and went into this convenience store to get something to drink and a snack. When I asked if I could use the bathroom, the old man behind the counter asked me if I was in trouble."

Doc nodded his head, mentally taking in every word she said.

"I told him I wasn't in trouble, but I did need a place to stay. He gave me five dollars and said it was enough to take the city bus to the address of a women's shelter and that I should ask for Mabel. Tell her Silas sent you, he'd said." Bree took a long breath shaking her head. "I was so scared when I walked into that house. Mabel immediately hugged me and took me into her fold, she was so kind to me. She said I would have to share a room with another girl, Victoria, but that she was close to my age."

"That must have been somewhat comforting having a room with another girl, feeling like you weren't alone," he said. Bree just nodded.

"Those first few days, I didn't want to leave my room. Mabel, she was so patient. She would bring me my meals, and sit and talk with me for hours and hours. When I asked her to help me find a job for the summer, she immediately took me back to the convenience store where the old man, Silas, had helped."

"He gave me a job and a purpose to get up every day. She would ask me every day how I was doing, and every day we would talk. I met this really nice policeman, Officer Kelly, who used to come in every morning for his coffee. He would come to the shelter to check on me and make sure I was doing okay."

"It's always nice to have a cop as a friend," grinned Doc. Bree smiled, nodding.

"The family I was staying with, and Mabel, didn't like him much. They said he was a dirty cop, but he never showed me anything but kindness. When I went off to college that next year, he paid for my deposits in my off-campus apartment, helped me move everything."

"Not Mabel?" asked Doc, somewhat surprised.

"No, no. I can't remember why really, she just said she couldn't come that day. Anyway, he helped me move, and then I got a job at a local coffee shop and one in the university book store. I saw Mabel on and off after that, but not as much. She was always busy with the girls at the shelter."

"What about Victoria?" asked Doc.

"Hmmm? Oh, you know I don't know whatever became of her. One day she was there, and the next she was gone. It wasn't uncommon. Mabel just said she'd moved on." Doc smiled at her as the bus came to a halt outside the visitor's center for the Canadian side of Niagara Falls.

"What about the family you were staying with? What were they like?" asked Doc, curiously digging a little deeper.

"You know, I didn't know them well. They stuck to themselves upstairs. There was a door out of the basement apartment to the street level, so I didn't have to see them much. They had a lot of visitors go in and out of that house, but I think he, Tim, that was his name, I think Tim was in software of some sort, and Helen ran his business from the house. They were just always there."

Doc just nodded, taking it all in.

As they stepped from the bus, he turned off the record button and sent the message. Shit was fucked up.

CHAPTER TWENTY-THREE

"Alright, everyone," said the tour guide through the bullhorn. "We'll be splitting you up on the boats. Please grab a raincoat and find a spot on the decks to get your perfect viewing spot, and of course, spectacular photographs." The crowds laughed, and Doc smiled down at Bree, glad that she was enjoying herself, her mind off Alicia if only for a few hours.

"It's so beautiful," said Bree, staring at the falls with awe. "It could be really romantic if we weren't surrounded by two hundred other people." Doc nodded, laughing.

"Baby, anywhere you are is romantic for me."

"Do they teach you to say romantic stuff like that in the Rangers?" she asked, eyeing him suspiciously. Doc laughed, tilting his head back.

"I promise, gorgeous, that is the last thing they teach you as a Ranger. Shooting, fighting, jumping out of planes, blowing shit up, that's all part of the curriculum definitely."

The thunderous sounds of millions of gallons of water falling over the grand horseshoe-shaped falls were mesmerizing. The freezing spray pelted the skin on their faces like tiny ice bullets. The boat captain droned on about the history of the falls and their discovery, which seemed stupid since you can't discover something that was already there. And, of course, he had to get in a dig about how the Canadian side of the falls was far more spectacular than the American side.

"Alright, everyone, wave at your American friends in our American partner boat," laughed the guide. Bree smiled, waving at the other boat just like the others. The smiling faces of tourists waved at them, obviously having received the same direction from their guide. Shaking hands covered in wool, wiggled at them, and Bree laughed. She raised her own hand to wave and stilled in mid-air, tilting her head slightly to get a better view of the other boat.

Standing against the railing with two men was Mabel. Her distinctive white hair and purple leopard wool coat making her stand out against the others. She had a look of frustration, her hands flailing about as she spoke rapidly to the two men.

"What... why is she... ?" she whispered. Doc looked at Bree and connected with her eyes, following their path to the other boat.

"What the fuck?" Leaning against the railing of the boat, separated by a few feet from the other tourists were Krevnyv and an unidentified man talking to Mabel.

"How did she get on that side of the falls?" asked Bree. "And more importantly, who are those men she's speaking with? She looks mad." Doc immediately gripped her shoulders, turning her to face in the other direction, her back now to Mabel, Krevnyv and the other man.

"Honey, listen to me. Don't look back at the boat, okay?" Bree nodded. Doc casually pulled her hood up and over her very identifiable head of red hair. He positioned his phone up to take a photo.

"A selfie? Now?" asked Bree with a shocked expression.

"Just smile, baby," he said, lifting the phone. She immediately noticed that it wasn't them in the view. It was Mabel and the two other men.

"Who are they?" she asked.

"I don't think we should talk here," he said, kissing her, turning her once more from the line of sight of the other boat.

"Jack? What the hell is going on here? Why would Mabel be on an American boat when she was on the Canadian side of the falls?" Jack casually walked toward the stairs leading to the bottom level of the boat.

"Let's get some coffee, okay?"

Bree nodded, but she was so filled with pain and confusion, her head was literally swimming. She wanted desperately to talk. To try and understand what they'd just seen, but Doc seemed intent on not speaking, only portraying the doting boyfriend.

As the boat docked, the guide told them they would have an hour to explore the area around the falls, take photos, and of course, spend their American dollars in the Canadian gift shop. Doc pulled Bree gently away from the crowd, down the steps toward one of the look-out vistas.

"Jack..." she started. He held his finger to his lips and looked at her, shaking his head. When they finally reached the furthest point, he turned to look at her. "What the hell is going on?"

"Honey, how much do you really know about Mabel?"

"What? I... I've known her for almost twenty years now." Doc sucked on his bottom lip and looked back toward the steps.

"I know that, baby. I need you to tell me what you really know about her. The shelter, how old were the women in this shelter?" Bree stepped back as if he'd struck her. No. No, he couldn't be serious about this. What was he implying?

"What the hell are you asking?" Her mitten-covered hands were fisted at her sides.

"Bree, those men she was talking to on the boat, one is a Russian criminal who we know is trafficking young girls. The other is a well-known buyer of flesh. How old were the other girls, Bree?"

"I..." she shook her head and looked across the falls to the American flag flapping in the cold north wind. "They were young like me. Teenagers..." she said in a whisper.

"All of them? The whole time you were there?" She nodded. The sound of a text message pinged on his phone, and he looked down.

Get out of there now

"Okay, baby, let's go."

"I don't think so." Doc heard the distinctive sound of a pistol cocking and stared at the very angry face of Mabel Beckstein.

CHAPTER TWENTY-FOUR

"Mabel? What are you doing? What the hell is going on here?" asked Bree. Doc stepped in front of her, blocking her body from Mabel, but the older woman only laughed.

"He is quite protective, isn't he, dear?" said Mabel. Bree said nothing, a tear falling from her eye. "I know you tried desperately to hide yourselves on the boat, but it's really quite difficult when you're both rather Amazonian, and of course, Bree with all that red hair.

"You two are going to take a little drive with me and my friends. Now, it will most likely be one-way, but then again, you've probably already guessed that. Didn't you, my big friend." She stared at Doc, who said nothing, only glaring at the woman.

"How did you get on this side of the falls so quickly?" asked Bree. Mabel just smiled at the girl. She'd had so much promise. Tall, beautiful, smart, she was going to be the one Mabel would keep and get her to help bring others in if the bids on her weren't high enough. She'd fucked it all up with that summer job.

"Oh, Bree, you really are still just a naïve little girl, aren't you?" said Mabel, laughing at her. Bree was suddenly pissed as she tried to step around Doc, but he wasn't having it. "Up the stairs."

"I don't think so," said Doc.

"Up the stairs or Bree dies, and since I suspect she's more than just a quick fuck, you'll do as you're told," said Mabel. She stared at Bree. "Finally got over your little phobia of intimacy, did you, dear? No longer see stepdaddy's hands and cock when you fuck someone? I'll bet he has a nice one too. Does he? Never mind, that's rhetorical. I do think he's probably taught you some things that would have been useful for me when you were younger, but alas, you're past your prime for what I need."

Bree felt the sting of tears, but more than that, she saw Doc's face as a red dot appeared on her chest. Panicked, his eyes darted around the area to see if he could spot the shooter.

"Uh, uh, uh. Don't do anything stupid, Jack Harris. We just want to have a chat with you, that's all."

"Fine. I'll come. Let Bree go."

"That's not how this works, handsome. You know that." Doc waited, trying to decide if there was another way out.

"What is it you want?" asked Doc, staring at the short woman. He should have listened to his instincts. They'd only met briefly in the lobby, but something about the woman didn't sit well with Doc, and he should have listened. Fuck!

"I want to know what the girl said to you last night," she said, smiling at the couple. Bree's face turned ashen, any sense of loyalty to this woman now gone.

"You… you were a part of that… you…"

"Jesus, Bree! This is really getting exhausting, okay? Both of you, up the stairs to the dark blue van."

"No! No, I won't go with you, you monster! How could you allow them to do that to a child?" yelled Bree. Before Bree could get her answers, two men stepped behind Mabel, both with guns tucked slightly beneath their coats but definitely allowing Doc and Bree to see.

"I think you should change your mind," said Mabel. Doc nodded at her. Gripping Bree's hand, they followed the woman and her two goons up the stairs, only to be greeted by an exuberant and exasperated tour guide.

"Where have you two been? We've been waiting! Get on the bus, please," he screeched, waving his arms toward the buses.

"I'm sorry, but my friends and I are taking a private tour from here," said Mabel.

"A private tour? That's highly irregular. I have to keep count of everyone on that bus, and when someone doesn't return, I'm in trouble." He waved his hands up and down. Mabel stuffed two one-hundred-dollar bills in his pocket and smiled.

"There you are, young man. This should alleviate any issues you might have in responding to questions." He looked at that old woman and then back at the two men.

"Fine." Bree wanted to scream out for him to stop, but Doc squeezed her fingers and gave a quick shake of his head. The goon squad pushed them toward the van. Once out of view inside the closed van doors, they zip tied their hands while Mabel took the front passenger seat.

"Where are you taking us?" asked Doc.

"Just for a little ride," said Mabel. "What did the girl say?"

"The girl had a name," said Bree through clenched teeth. "Alicia, it was Alicia. Did you even fucking know her name?!" Mabel said nothing, not even giving Bree any indication she'd heard her, she just continued to stare at Doc.

"Nothing, she said nothing. She was too beaten and too far gone. By the time we got to her, she was dying." Doc tried to speak without emotion, without letting his anger rise to the surface. He called on every ounce of training he possessed to remain calm.

"Really?" said Mabel. "Well, now, that's a shame. It seems we took you for no reason at all." A sprig of hope blossomed in Bree's chest and was just as quickly squashed as they pulled into a huge empty field, where the trailer from an eighteen-wheeler was parked by itself.

"Oh God," whispered Bree. "Why, Mabel?"

"Because trying to save pathetic lost souls like you is fucking exhausting, that's why." She screamed into Bree's face. Bree tried not to cry, really she did, but she felt the sting of hot tears coming to the surface. "I wasted the first twenty years of my life trying to help girls like you. Women from abused marriages, making shit for money."

"But... but you were abused," said Bree.

"Yep, and I fucking shot that asshole. Left him to die in the shithole of a motel I found him in, getting his dick sucked by a twenty-dollar whore. Then decided that was too good for him. I dragged his ass to the car and threw him off a bridge. That was exhilarating, I have to tell you! I left him there and made my way to D.C.. Lots of perverts there, if you didn't know that." Mabel laughed.

"I stayed in a shelter for a year. Then they hired me, and I got a piece of garbage apartment where it was mostly hookers and drug dealers for neighbors. Came home one night to find a well-known Congressman banging the thirteen-year-old next door in the hall of all the stupid things. I tried to bribe him. He threatened to kill me. I fucked him instead, but then he offered me a deal we could both live with."

"You're sick. You're despicable," said Bree. Mabel slapped her face hard. Doc tried to crawl into the front seat but paid for it with a punch on the side of the head from goon number one. Bree's tears fell freely.

"He set me up in that little house. All I had to do was find pathetic little runaways. Unhappy teenagers willing to do anything to defy Mommy and Daddy. A little lure of a trip to the mall, wine, parties. It was easy. Until you. I got you that fucking job at the Stop and Shop so clients could see you, bid on you."

"You did what?" Bree couldn't breathe. Her heart literally felt as though it were beating through her chest. She looked over at Doc, who seemed so calm she wanted to scream.

"Yea, well, you pissed on that one for me. Made friends with that fucking cop on the first damn day. He made sure he was in there every morning watching you – on weekends, days off – it didn't matter. Even caught him following you home a few times. Prick was suspicious of me for some reason. He didn't have anything on me, but he sure as hell tried. You always seemed to make friends with the people I needed you to stay away from." She eyed Doc up and down with a leer.

Bile rose in Bree's throat. Sgt. Kelly had been killed in the line of duty when she was in college. Some apparent drug dealer stabbed him in an alley, leaving a wife and two sons.

"Did you… did you kill him?" asked Bree.

"Me? No, dear, I don't get my hands dirty in that way. But I made damned sure someone else did the job. Seems he finally did find something on me."

"I hate you," whispered Bree. "I will never forgive you. Never."

"Understood," said Mabel, looking forlorn, nodding her head mockingly. "Not that I give a shit. Take their coats." The door opened, and both were pulled from the van, the freezing winds from the lake assaulting the bare skin of their faces.

"We'll have to untie them to take the coats off," said goon number two.

"Cut them off, you fucking idiot!" He nodded at the old woman and pulled out a knife, slicing the sleeves of Bree's coat first, all the way to her shoulders and then down the back, ripping it from her body. The cold air rushed her, stealing the breath from her body. "Take their phones and crush them."

As goon number one cut Doc's coat, he took his chance, head butting the man so hard the crunching sound of cartilage filled the air, dropping him to his knees. Mabel never even hesitated. Pulling her weapon, she fired into his thigh.

"NO!" screamed Bree. "No!"

"Leave them. I really am sorry it's come to this, Bree. You should have just stayed away." Bree watched as Mabel and the goons took off in the van. Kneeling beside Doc, she kissed him, crying.

"Please, don't die, Jack, please. I love you..." Doc maneuvered onto his elbows, sitting up.

"I'm not gonna die, baby, and I love you too. The cold is helping the blood to slow. They didn't hit anything vital. It just hurts like fuck. Help me stand," he said, leaning against her. She placed her elbow in the crook of his arm and stood, both leaning against the other.

"Now what?" asked Bree.

"Now we get the fuck out of here."

CHAPTER TWENTY-FIVE

Doc walked toward the tractor-trailer. Walking around it, he used his bound, clasped hands to feel the edges of the metal until he found the spot he needed. Rubbing his wrists back and forth along the sharp exposed steel, the zip tie broke free.

"Come over here, baby," he said to Bree. She was already shivering violently from the cold temperatures. Bree wasn't quite tall enough to reach the metal, so Jack lifted her, placing the zip tie around the curved metal edge. "Gently rub back and forth, honey."

Bree nodded, tears falling at an alarming rate as she rubbed back and forth, the tie finally snapping. Doc pulled her to his chest, encasing her in his arms, his big hands brusquely rubbing up and down her back. They both had two layers of clothing on, but it wasn't nearly enough for the temperatures in the open field.

"We have to get out of here," he whispered into her hair. Bree nodded, pulling back.

"I'm sorry. This is my fault," said Bree.

"It's not your fault, baby. You had no idea." He hugged her again. "Baby, the text I got as Mabel took us, it was the team. They found out about her. She's been feeding girls to Krevnyv for almost twenty years now. Krevnyv buys the girls, trains them, and then sells them to predators."

"Oh God, I think I'm going to be sick," she said, bending at the waist. Doc rubbed her back, looking around the field. He listened, thinking he heard something, and then tilted his head again.

"Did you hear that?" he said.

"Wh-what? I... yea... a cow, I think."

"That's right, honey, and where there are cows, there are farms." He grabbed her hand and then looked at the trailer sitting in the field. "Let's see if there's something in there we can use to keep warm."

Bree nodded as they walked to the rear of the trailer. Pulling on the handle, Doc pulled the first door open, shoving it back and then reached for the second one to do the same. He thought he saw shadows in the trailer but couldn't be sure.

He stepped up onto the lift and took only two steps before stopping.

"What is it?" asked Bree. "What's in there?"

Doc took a step back, shaking his head. Bree started to step into the trailer, but he waved her back, still shaking his head.

"Jack?" she whispered.

"It's bodies..."

CHAPTER TWENTY-SIX

There was no answer to their knocking at the farmhouse, so Jack did what he needed to. He broke a window. He carefully stepped through each room, his leg throbbing from the pain of the bullet. Bree found the bathroom, searching the cabinets for a first aid kit. She came out with everything she knew they would need.

"Pour the alcohol over the wound," directed Doc. He winced as she let the fiery liquid cover the now bloody wound. "Now, do the same with those tweezers." He was breathless from the pain, but it wasn't nearly as agonizing as some of his other bullet wounds had been.

"I'm so sorry, Jack," tears filled her eyes as she worked, but Doc only reached out, cupping her chin and pulling her toward him, kissing her lips sweetly.

"No one I'd rather get shot with, beautiful." She smiled up at him and laughed. "I need you to try and get the bullet out, Bree." She nodded and felt around the opening.

"I... I think I can actually see it," she said.

"Yea, she shot me in the fleshy part of the thigh, so I think we might get lucky here. I'd do it myself, but I quit my yoga classes a year ago, and my flexibility is for shit." Bree smiled up at him and his attempt at humor. She tried to do it without causing too much pain, but no matter what she did... this was going to hurt like fuck. After a few minutes, she pulled the bullet out and smiled, his face pale and gray.

"You did it, gorgeous," he said breathlessly. Doc wiped away the excess blood and began to wrap the wound. Stitching wasn't going to happen here. He'd worry about that later. He looked around the kitchen and spotted a wall phone. Lifting it, he was pleased to hear that it was still active and dialed, making the call to Ghost.

"Where the fuck are you?! I sent you an urgent fucking text and then nothing. Your locator on the phone is off. What the fuck, Doc!?" yelled Ghost.

"Nice to fucking talk to you too," said Doc. "We're in the middle of..." Bree handed him an electric bill with an address on it. "Grimsby. Mabel and two hired muscle took us from the tour group to a field. Took our coats, broke our phones, and shot me in the thigh."

"I'm sending Zulu and Whiskey now. Are you safe?" asked Ghost.

"We're in a farmhouse. Not sure where the owner is, but there's a trailer parked on what could be his property filled with the bodies of at least a dozen dead little girls." Ghost was quiet, practically silent on the other end of the phone.

"I'm getting too old for this," he whispered into the phone.

"How did you know about Mabel?" asked Doc.

"Ivan said he thought there was a woman helping Anton. When you saw Krevnyv in Toronto, it was just too much of a coincidence. I had Ace start checking on all the attendees of the conference. The only one that stood out was Mabel."

"Why?" asked Doc.

"She has no professional credentials. That alone wouldn't raise red flags except that the conference requires attendees to have a minimum of a master's in social work, nursing, or psychology. Ace checked the rosters for the classes. She wasn't signed up for any of them."

"She told Bree that she'd been luring girls through the house for years. Said she had an arrangement with a congressman," Doc watched as Bree scratched out a note on a piece of paper, wrapping a twenty-dollar bill inside. He could only smile at her for thinking of the owner of the house at a time like this.

"Do you think the girls in the trailer are the same ones who were shipped?" asked Ghost. Doc didn't want to answer with Bree sitting there, but he knew he had to.

"No. They've been dead at least two weeks. The cold has kept them from decomposing, but their bodies were used Ghost, fucking brutally used." He rubbed a hand over his face and sighed.

"Okay, listen. Can you find something warm to wear? I want you to get out of there just in case there's something going on with the farmer."

"Something warm to wear?" he said to Bree. She stood and started opening doors. A few minutes later, she came out with two men's parkas, a couple of sweaters, hats, and mittens. He smiled at her and nodded. Looking out the window, he spotted an old motorcycle leaning against the garage.

"I might be in luck," he said to Ghost, explaining his find and what their plan of action would be.

"Stick to Lakeshore Road. They're going to meet you at a diner near Oakville if you can make it that far."

"We'll make it." Doc hung up the phone. "Bree? Gotta go, baby." She came out of one of the back rooms, bundled up in the old coat.

"Will this help?" she said, holding out an old revolver. Doc raised his brows, grinning at her.

"Yea, yea, baby, that might help." Doc checked the weapon. It appeared to be clean and well cared for, the cylinders full. "Let's go, honey. I gotta hotwire a bike."

CHAPTER TWENTY-SEVEN

Pulling into the diner, Doc and Bree stepped off the old motorcycle, their faces frozen from the wind. Bree tried to keep her face buried into Doc's back, but it didn't seem to matter. Winter in Toronto on a motorcycle sucked.

They opened the door into the warmth of the restaurant and sucked in warm gulps of air. Whiskey and Zulu were seated in the corner. Both men rose, pulling first Bree and then Doc into a hug.

"Are you two okay?" asked Whiskey, eyeing them up and down. "Anything hurt?"

"I had a bullet in my thigh thanks to that old bitch, but my nurse here helped me dig it out." He smiled at Bree, who gave a pained expression. "We're good, brother. Any word on her whereabouts?" he asked, seeing Bree shift uncomfortably in her seat.

"No. CMP is headed out to the farm to recover the girls. They have a description and her passport information, but we both know Krevnyv has far-reaching fingers. If they want out of Canada, they'll get out."

"I'm going to use the ladies' room," said Bree, standing shakily from the booth. The men raised slightly, and she smiled.

"She's not handling it well," said Doc. "She trusted that woman, thought of her as a mentor, and it turns out she's a fucking flesh selling Madame of teenage girls. What about the other girls, the girls that were coming from Miami?"

"No word yet. Ivan is still trying to find them, but Krevnyv is really being tight-lipped about it," said Whiskey. "Ivan said before Krevnyv came to Toronto, he and his daughter had a huge argument. She accused him of exactly the things he was doing, loud and clear. Ivan said it also sounded like he was going to force his daughter to leave school, but he finally relented."

"You think he's going to fucking sell his own daughter?" asked Zulu.

"Maybe," said Whiskey, "or maybe he's grooming her for his role, and she doesn't want it. Either way, we may be forced to make contact with her at some point."

Bree came back to the table. Sitting next to Doc, she laced her fingers with his.

"I'm so sorry for all this trouble," she said to Whiskey and Zulu. "I should have seen what was happening with Mabel and the house. All these years, I'd go back there and not once, not once..."

"Not your fault, beautiful," said Whiskey. "Sometimes evil lifts its head in the most unusual places. We just need to get you and Doc home, and then we're gonna track this shit down."

"No."

All eyes turned, looking at the beautiful doctor. She shook her head, biting her lower lip, trying to fight back tears. Her red hair was a mess of tangles around her head, the flush from the cold the only color on her otherwise ghostly face.

"Honey..."

"No. I want to help find this woman, and then I want to be here when we free those young girls to help them."

"Bree," said Whiskey, "the CMP will control the situation. We'll have no jurisdiction in this matter. We're lucky they're letting us stay this long. We'll find Mabel, and then we'll find those girls with the help of the CMP and the FBI. They're delivering warrants now to her shelter in Arlington."

Bree continued to shake her head.

"Baby, he's right. We'll have to leave and head back to the States. We can try to help from there." She kept shaking her head, tears now streaming down her face. The waitress stepped to the table and poured them all more coffee. Seeing Bree look so sad, she smiled.

"Can I get you something else, honey? Are you okay?" she asked, eyeing the three large men suspiciously.

"We've just really had a rough afternoon," said Doc. "Got stranded out at the falls and had to walk for miles in the cold and then got some pretty bad news."

"Oh, wow, that stinks," she said, smiling at the table. "Seems to be a run on that lately." Zulu looked up at the woman.

"What do you mean?"

"Oh, well, there was a young girl come through here a couple nights ago. She was all bruised and bloody, said she got in a fight with her boyfriend. I didn't believe her, really, but teenagers come in here all the time headed to the border. You know, sneak away from the parents and make their way to the States or from the States. Asked if I should call the police for her, and she was pretty determined to run if I did. I never push but always call for help if they ask."

"What happened to her?" he asked.

"Gave her enough money to get the bus into Toronto. That's all she wanted. Asked her if I could call someone for her, and she said she had no one. Let me know if you folks need anything else." She started to walk away, but Zulu gently grabbed her wrist.

"Ma'am, this is important. Did the girl give you a name?" The waitress nodded.

"Yea, Alicia. She said her name was Alicia."

CHAPTER TWENTY-EIGHT

"Where are the doctor and her biker friend?" asked Anton, staring at the woman he both loathed and needed.

"We took care of them," said Mabel, smiling at the big Russian. "Left them both without their coats, tied up in a field in the middle of nowhere, even shot the biker in the leg. They won't last out there."

Anton nodded but still didn't have his answers. This woman didn't know these men like he did. They weren't ordinary bikers. They were trained in ways that she could never possibly understand. He'd seen what they could do against the Warriors, and even more so, the balls they'd shown just by meeting with him and defying him at every turn.

"Where is the next shipment?" she asked. He looked up at the woman, her casual inquiry unsettling him. She'd been trying to take on bigger roles within their little enterprise for a year now. He needed to make her understand that he was in charge, not her.

"It's been turned back," he said casually.

"Turned back!?" she yelled, standing.

"Do not yell at me," said Anton through clenched teeth. "The girl being found ruined everything for all of us. Had you controlled that situation better, we would not be in this predicament. The mounted police are checking everything that comes across the border right now, opening cargo holds, searching trucks. We cannot bring the girls through here."

Mabel paced the room. This was supposed to be her last haul. These girls would yield a cool hundred thousand for her share alone. With that money, she'd finally be able to retire to her little place in the Caribbean.

"What about the buyers? What did you tell them, and where did you send the girls if they're not here?" she asked.

"The buyers were notified that there would be a change in venue. They understood, and in fact, appreciated our diligence in making sure it was a safe environment for them. As for where the girls are… nowhere yet. They are headed back south until I can decide what to do with them."

Mabel was frustrated with Anton. He'd always believed he was the head of the operation, when in fact, it was her. Originally, she'd had her arrangement with the congressman, but when he died three years ago, she needed someone else to step in with the funding. Anton was more than willing to partner with her. But he needed to know that she was in charge, not him.

"I have a second place in Virginia. The other house will be under surveillance now. We have to assume that somehow they know who I am. But no one knows about the second place. It's an old farmhouse, lots of bedrooms with locks," she smiled. Anton nodded at the woman.

She'd served her usefulness, but her demands lately were more than he wanted in his life. Anton thought of his own daughter back in Washington, D.C., headed to law school this year. He'd given in to her indulgences for too many years now. This was the last before he would deliver her to Omar as promised. After that, she'd be out of his hair and become someone else's problem.

Although he couldn't prove it, he was certain the little bitch had somehow contributed to his wife and son being killed. Maybe he should just turn her over to the bidders now? No, he didn't want any heat right now, and Katarina was notorious for creating chaos wherever she went. Let her finish her studies and think she was holding all the cards.

"Anton? Anton? Do you want to divert the girls to the farmhouse? I can make it across the border the hard way. I'll get to Buffalo and drive down from there. I could be back in DC in three or four days."

Anton looked out the window of the luxury penthouse apartment owned by one of his many corporations. Corporations that no one knew of. He stared at the lights of downtown Toronto, the snow still heavy on the ground.

"Yes. Go back. I'll arrange for the girls to be brought to you for safekeeping. If we can hold off for a few weeks, let everything die down a bit, perhaps I can hold the sale somewhere locally." Mabel nodded, leaving him alone with his thoughts.

It would take some walking and sleight of hand, but she would make it across the border and back home. Taking the elevator to the parking garage, she thought of the expression on Bree's face when she figured out Mabel's true occupation. There was such a look of shock and pain she almost felt sorry for her. Almost.

The truth was, Bree had been the one that got away. She couldn't get to her while the cop was hanging around. That asshole made his presence known from day one. Bree had no clue what was happening, but he made sure she was protected at every turn.

Then when she went off to college, she was always surrounded by people, professors, other students, and of course, the people she worked with. Leaving college, she'd gone to Baltimore for a while and then to the little fucking town in the middle of nowhere. Now she wasn't worth a red cent to her. She was too old, too tall, and well, too plump for most of her buyers. It didn't matter. She and the handsome biker were dead and no longer her problem.

"Where to Ms. Beckstein?" asked goon number one.

"Home."

CHAPTER TWENTY-NINE

"Whiskey?" said Ghost. "I think you and Zulu need to pay a visit to Katarina Krevnyv. See how she responds to your questions about her father. Maybe she knows something and will tell us." Whiskey nodded, an expression of uncertainty and something else Ghost couldn't quite put his finger on.

"Not Zulu – just me. He'll scare the shit out of her," he said, smiling at his friend as Zulu flipped him the bird.

"Doc? How is Bree settling in back home?" he asked.

"She's okay, frightened as you can imagine. I'm staying with her for the time being until my townhouse is done. She just can't seem to come to grips with the woman who saved her and the woman who's been selling girls to predators." Doc looked sad and tired.

"How's the leg? And don't give me any fucking bullshit." Doc grinned at his friend.

"It's fine, really. The pistol was only a small .38, and Bree did a great job of removing the bullet. I'll have a nice scar since I waited too long to get the stitches, but it's fine. I promise, Ghost." His friend nodded and looked around the room.

"Ace? What do we have?" Ace turned down the lights and pressed the button on the projector.

"Mabel Ruth Beckstein, formerly Cranston, married Ralph Beckstein in 1968. Ralph was a steelworker in Pittsburgh. Lost his job shortly after they were married and started drinking... a lot, according to police records. The first time he hit Mabel, he broke her jaw. Seems Ralph didn't just work in the steel mills. He had hands of steel, a former fighter."

"Christ!" said Zulu under his breath.

"Neighbors would call saying they could hear screaming and crying, but when the police would arrive, Mabel would always just say she fell. 1960s and '70s, the cops didn't do much with domestic abuse. On her last known emergency room visit, she was not only beaten but raped. She refused to give the police a statement, and they released her."

"A few days later, an officer showed up to check on her, and she was gone, the apartment empty. The neighbors said she left with two suitcases and hadn't seen her or the husband. About three weeks later, Ralph's body washed up on the Allegheny, a bullet in his brain."

"Now, Mabel makes it to Arlington and starts working for a shelter, the same one she was staying at. By all accounts, she was a calming force for the women, helped them, was kind, compassionate, everything you would want. About twenty years into her time at the shelter, she came in and said she was going to start a home for abuse victims."

"Just like that?" asked Doc.

"Just like that."

"You know, she said she got the funding from a congressman," said Doc.

"Yea, Congressman Matthew Renfrew. He was in office almost forty years, died about three years ago from natural causes. Married, two children, six grandchildren. When he died, the feds served a warrant for his computers on suspicion of misdirecting funds. Instead, they found thousands of photos of young women in various stages of undress."

"And why the fuck was that never in the media?" asked Whiskey.

"Seems Mrs. Renfrew is highly thought of in Washington. She has a, ummm, delicate constitution, and no one wanted to upset her. What a fucking joke, right?" They all nodded. "Anyway, the computers are wiped clean, the fucking feds not even caring where the photos of the girls came from. That's where Anton enters. He'd been buying from Renfrew, and indirectly, from Mabel for years."

"Mabel needed financial backing and contacts. She could supply the girls, but she couldn't get the bidders and couldn't transport them. By accident, she somehow figures out that Anton was a frequent dinner companion to the Congressman and puts two and two together that he was buying from them."

"According to my source at the bureau, they believe that Mabel, Renfrew, and now Anton have supplied more than three thousand girls in the last twenty years to overseas buyers. She has a network of people that help her get the girls. A big buyer is Omar Khanaman. Khanaman is a low-level sheik in the Arab world but has millions in family oil money. The bureau says they have a taped conversation between him and Anton indicating that he has a keen interest in the daughter."

"What?!" yelled Whiskey. Ghost looked at his friend and then back at Ace, who raised an eyebrow. "We can't let that fucking animal sell his own daughter."

"I agree, brother," said Ghost, "which is why I want you to speak to her. See if she'll give us any information at all on Daddy. Offer her protection."

"The house in Arlington was searched. Two girls who were living there, both underage, said nothing had happened yet, but Mabel told them she wanted them to go to a party with her. They've been moved to another facility, and the files have been removed, but it will take the bureau ages to get through them all."

"Shit!"

"Don't lose hope," smiled Ace. "I was able to hack into her computers before they got to them. She was pretty good about not keeping anything in digital format, which leads me to believe there must be something in paper form. I did, however, see several e-mails back and forth between her and Krevnyv about meetings. No details, but it's enough to link them."

"On a somber note..."

"That wasn't fucking somber?" asked Gunner.

"I wish, brother. The girls in the trailer outside of Toronto? Most were from Mexico shipped all the way across country into Canada. The abuse, it was too much, more than enough to kill them. They've only done autopsies on three, and already, they know they were raped by at least fifteen different men, vaginally and anally. Not one of them wore a condom. DNA is everywhere, but so far, no hits. They all had multiple broken bones. Two were punched directly over their hearts hard enough to stop them."

"Jesus Christ, have mercy on those poor children," whispered Skull. "Someone knew what they were doing. It was a game to them." His fists clenched and unclenched as Ace told the details.

"Did any have family?" asked Ghost.

"Yea, most did. So far, six have been identified as having gone to the same school in Mexico City. The others they're still working on identifying."

"What a fucking mess!" Ghost stood as Ace turned the lights on in the meeting room once again. He paced behind the chairs of the men he called brothers, touching a shoulder now and then, just to let them know he was here for them.

"What about the teacher?" asked Whiskey.

"Yea, that piece of shit," said Ace. "Edward Stewart, forty-two, single, never been married. He owned a home out near Falls Church. He would get the girls to come and dance for his buddies. If the girls took their clothes off, he'd pay them five hundred dollars. If they let the men kiss them, another five hundred, and if they allowed the men to touch them in any way, they'd give them a thousand dollars."

"When the girls were exceptionally pretty, he would take photos. Two girls at the middle school said they were at one of the parties and refused to do anything but dance for the men. They said it made them feel dirty."

"Smart girls," said Zulu.

"Yea, except Mr. Stewart then made their lives a living hell. Threatened that if they went to the police, he would tell their parents what they did. The girls said they heard others say that the men would penetrate with their fingers but didn't know of anyone who was raped."

"Were they checking them? Seeing if they were virgins?" asked Tango. Ace nodded.

"Most likely. He's now in federal custody, and I've requested permission to interview him. We know that the shipment Ivan told us about never made it into Canada. He thinks that Anton sent it back into the States. We just don't know where. If Anton is still working with Mabel, then maybe she has somewhere else to send the girls."

"Any clues?" asked Whiskey. Ace shook his head.

"Maybe Bree would know of some other place?" asked Whiskey. Doc looked at his friend and shrugged.

"Wait, Alicia, she kept saying 'the falls.' Maybe that's what she was referring to, Falls Church." The others all looked deep in thought, and Doc stood. "Let me get Bree. She's out there with Grace. I'll ask her to come in."

CHAPTER THIRTY

"How are you feeling?" asked Bree, looking at the small baby bump on Grace.

"I'm good, honey, tire easily, but I'm good. The better question is, how are you? This must be so difficult for you, Bree." She nodded at her friend, looking at the crowd of people in the club this evening.

"You know, I spent almost twenty years believing in that woman. I thought she saved me, that she gave me the chance I needed to find a life. Little did I know she was planning on taking the life I thought I'd found and selling me. Worse than that, right under my nose, she was selling other young women."

"Oh, sweetie, you couldn't possibly have known that. You were a child yourself, Bree," said Grace, holding her hand.

"I know. I know you're right, but I was thinking about all the girls who were my roommates when I was there. Victoria, she was the first. She was this beautiful girl with long blonde hair and bright blue eyes. One day she was there, the next she was gone. Mabel said she'd found a home, that she'd moved on. What a fucking joke!" yelled Bree a little too loudly. The crowd hushed, and she blushed, looking at Grace, who gave her a small smile.

"So many girls. Victoria. Beth. Analise. Keisha. So many," she whispered.

"Bree, you're going to make yourself sick thinking about it, honey. Listen, you're doing what you should be doing. It seems pretty prophetic to me that you are now spending a life helping victims of the very thing you were caught in the middle of." Bree nodded at her.

"I know in my heart you're right, Grace, but it's my head I can't seem to get to catch up. I mean, I'm an intelligent woman. How did I not see in almost twenty years the evil in that woman's heart?"

"I can't answer that," said Grace. "By the same token, how could I not see the evil in the heart and soul of my ex-husband? How could I not see his intent to kill our children? My parents? I don't think that kind of evil just lies on the surface, Bree. I think some people become so adept at hiding it we just struggle with identifying it. We become so used to certain behavior that we accept them as normal until something like this happens, and then we say that was abnormal."

"I know you're right. I know. I just..."

"I know, sweetie. I get it. Listen, it seems to me you've got the best person in the world to talk to. Doc. He sure looks at you like you're the only woman in the room, and I know for a fact you feel the same way about him. Just take your time and talk to him."

"I was thinking," said Bree, "about the girls in that truck somewhere. They're probably scared and cold and hungry. They had no clue what they were doing, and yet somehow they lured them to a party or into a car, and now they find themselves trapped. I need to figure out a way to talk to schools about this more."

"I think that's a great place to put your energy," said Grace. "Listen, we talk to our kids about everything. Drugs, alcohol, even sex, or at least I did. But I can tell you this, I don't ever recall having a lengthy conversation with my girls about child predators or being careful going to a party where the people there were older. I probably mentioned it but didn't emphasize the importance of the talks. I mean, who would think to have those conversations in detail."

"I think sometimes parents think if they don't talk about those things, then they don't exist," said Bree. "I know for a fact a lot of my clients ended up in their situations because of that very thing. I've had dozens of women over the years who were raped or sexually abused by family members because their parents were too frightened to speak with them about healthy sexual desires, what was appropriate and with whom. I'm not saying it was the parents' fault, but what if they did have those conversations?" Grace nodded again.

"I know that if my mother had only spoken to me, I would have known that what Carl was doing to me as a child was wrong. And had she believed me, I wouldn't be in this situation now... afraid, filled with rage and concern for a truck full of girls."

"Yea," said Doc, walking up behind her kissing her neck, "but I might not have met you, and that, beautiful, would be completely unacceptable." Bree turned in his embrace, kissing his jaw and inhaling the scent of Doc.

"Are you boys done?" asked Grace.

"Not quite yet. We'd like to talk to you if you feel up to it," he said to Bree. She exhaled a long slow breath and nodded.

"Let's do it."

CHAPTER THIRTY-ONE

It wasn't the first time Bree had been in the meeting room, but it was the first time she'd been in there with so many men. Typically, the weekly meetings, or church as they sometimes called it, had the officers or top men in the MC. Today, it had almost everyone who was available.

"Hi, Bree," said Ghost, standing. "Thanks for joining us, honey. We'd like to ask you some questions about your time with Mabel and then about running into her in Toronto. You feel up to it?"

"I'm good, Ghost, really. Thank you all for working on this, for trying to help those lost girls," she said. She took the seat next to Doc and stared at the men.

"Good, good, we'd like for you to tell us the story of meeting Mabel and then every detail you can from there, okay?" she gave a slight nod and took in a deep breath.

"I think it might be important for you to understand how I got there because thinking on it now, I believe I was targeted. I was a runaway. Originally from Marion, Ohio. My mom was a drunk and went through husbands almost as fast as bottles. My stepfather, Carl, started touching me when I was seven."

There was a sharp and sudden shift in the room. She felt it before she saw it like the air had been sucked from the room, and a vice was wrapping around the remaining oxygen. Men sitting straighter, fists clenched, backs pressed against their chairs or the wall. Doc squeezed her hand.

"He enjoyed masturbating while I was on his lap. I didn't understand, but when I tried to tell my mother about it, I was punished. When I refused to sit on his lap, he would come in the bedroom and rub my legs while he did it. When I was sixteen, he tried to rape me. He didn't succeed, but I knew he would if I didn't leave, so I ran. I took a bus to Arlington, as far as my money would take me. I wandered from shelter to shelter for a few days, and then this convenience store owner referred me to Mabel."

"Did he refer her by name?" asked Ace. Bree thought for a moment.

"Yea, yea, he did. He said Mabel ran a shelter for girls. He didn't say women; he said girls. I remember after working there for a while that another girl was referred to Mabel by him as well."

The men all looked at one another again. The store owner had been a part of it as well, probably screening the girls.

"Anyway, I found Mabel, and she said I would be well taken care of. She put me in a room with another girl, Victoria. We were together for almost a month, and then one day, Victoria just disappeared. By that time, I had a job at that same convenience store. I came home from work one day, and she was gone. Mabel said she'd moved on, but she was seventeen like me, almost eighteen." She shook her head.

"Honey, the man at the convenience store, did he ever touch you?" asked Ace.

"I, yes, I didn't remember that until just now. It was only one time. I had only been working a few days. I was stocking the shelves, and he came up behind me, telling me how pretty I was. He put his hand at my waist, and I tried to back up, but he just kept coming closer. The door opened and it was Officer Kelly, the man who'd protected me all those years.

"He never came after me again, but I remember Mabel and the family I was staying with trying to convince me that Kelly was a dirty cop, and I should stay away from him. I didn't, of course. He'd been nothing but kind to me, and if I'm being honest, I felt safer knowing he was there."

"What about other girls in the house, honey?" asked Ace.

"There were never more than four or five at a time. I always thought that was weird because she had space for double that. I know there was a need out there, but she didn't have more. When she found me the home to stay in, I still went back on occasion to check on Mabel. She would ask me to talk to the girls now and then, let them know they were safe, and everything was okay." Bree covered her mouth, tears springing to her eyes. The men all looked at her knowing what she'd just figured out.

"Oh God, oh God, she used me to convince those girls to stay, to make those girls..." She lowered her head to the table and sobbed, Doc rubbing small circles around her back. A few minutes later, Hawk entered with a glass of whiskey. She nodded, sipping the burning liquor as it warmed her body.

"How could I have not seen this?" she whispered. They didn't have an answer and didn't attempt to respond. "When I... when I went off to college, Officer Kelly, he'd made sergeant by then, he helped me move into my apartment. He even came to see me a few times. Mabel never did. She always said she couldn't leave the house. When I was in my first year of the master's program, I received word that he'd been killed in the line of duty. It was like my heart had been ripped from my chest. I graduated the following year and just couldn't fathom working in the city after that."

"I took a job in Baltimore with a non-profit, counseling families for a few years while working on my PhD. Mabel said I was wasting my time, and I should come work with her. She kept saying she would pay me double what I was making. I couldn't understand how that was possible. I know now, but then..."

The men all nodded their heads.

"When I knew I was going to the conference in Toronto, I reached out to her to see if she would be there. She acted surprised at first, almost like attending a conference like that would be unheard of, and I understand now why. I didn't tell her about Jack. When I saw her in the lobby and hugged her, I said... I said, 'I have someone special I want you to meet.' I said, 'he's important to me.' She didn't say anything at first. She was nice to Jack, but later that day, before we left for the event at Casa

Loma, she said she thought he was a mistake. That I needed to dump him."

Doc stiffened next to her, anger filling his bones for the old woman and her maliciousness. She'd ruined hundreds of lives and attempted to ruin theirs as well.

"I told her… I told her I was in love," she said, smiling up at them all. They all smiled back.

"You sure, beautiful?" asked Zulu. "I'm always here if you change your mind." Even Doc laughed at Zulu's attempts to lighten the mood.

"I asked her if she would be at the event, and she said she had something else to do. That was the last time I saw her before the falls, and you all know what happened there. All she wanted to know was what Alicia told us the night before."

"And did she say anything?" asked Ghost. Bree shook her head.

"Not to me, but I didn't get close to her. I ran for help, and Doc took over from there." All eyes turned to Doc as he remembered that night. The girl's body had been so broken and torn, flesh cut open everywhere, blood and bruises covering her small frame.

"No, she said 'the falls' a few times, but I can only assume now that she was talking about the trailer near the falls or Falls Church. I asked her who did that to her and she just said, 'lots of men.' My guess is maybe they were going to leave her in that trailer or did thinking she was dead. Somehow she made it to that diner and then to Toronto."

"Did she know that you were going to a conference in Toronto, Bree?" asked Ace.

"I, yes, I mentioned it to her at our last session, the one where she ran," said Bree quietly. Ghost nodded at Doc, and he stood, pulling Bree with him.

"Thank you all for what you do," she said, turning to the group. "Whatever happens... these girls will need help, and I want to be here to help you. Not just now, but going forward." Ghost nodded and smiled at her.

As the couple left, the room became eerily silent. Bree had shed some light on what happened that they could definitely use to dig deeper, but Ghost knew their thoughts all went to Carl, her stepfather. Doc re-entered the room and looked at his teammates and brothers.

"I'll handle digging for more information here," said Ace. "I suggest two things. One, Whiskey and I head to D.C.. We get Whiskey to speak with Anton's daughter to see what she might know, and I'll try to get in and speak to the teacher. And two, Carl Sheffield still lives in Marion, Ohio, 871 Pinewood, Apartment 282, either you go, or I will."

CHAPTER THIRTY-TWO

Ace dropped Whiskey off near Georgetown, where he made his way toward the address they had on Katarina Krevnyv. He had seen the picture, but the data confirmed that she was twenty-two, almost twenty-three with a birthday in just a few days, five-foot-six, one hundred and sixteen pounds, blonde and blue-eyed. She had an undergraduate degree in criminal justice and was to attend Georgetown Law School in January.

The sprawling three-story Georgian townhome easily cost several million dollars, the neighborhood one of the finest in the D.C. area. Foreign cars lined the street, not a pathetic domestic brand in sight, although he had to smile at the custom-built motorcycle in the driveway of the house three over from Katarina.

He recognized every feature of the bike. The twin exhaust, custom chrome, tank with a soaring eagle on a red, white, and blue background; it was beautiful. He should know. He'd helped build that bike, and at fifty grand, it wasn't cheap.

The front door opened to a long, leggy blonde stepping onto the porch. She locked the door and made her way down the block to the train station. Interesting. Rich girl with a hot ride, and yet she takes the train.

Whiskey watched as the cascade of blonde hair swung back and forth down her back. Her tall body was lean like that of a dancer. She wore blue jeans with a small-heeled ankle boot; he couldn't see her top with the heavy wool coat, but she carried what he knew was a very expensive designer bag.

Standing several yards away, he watched as she waited for the train. She stepped into the third car, and he took the second one, still having her in his line of sight. A few stops later, she left the train heading to street level. Whiskey kept his distance, biding his time until he could be sure she was alone. She ducked into a coffee shop, and he waited outside, casually glancing at the magazines on the rack outside.

Katarina and her coffee came out a few minutes later, and she made her way onto campus. It was pretty dead for a university campus, and then it dawned on Whiskey that it was most likely winter break. He didn't attend college in the traditional way, but he knew enough to know kids were out pretty much after the first week of December.

He watched as she entered the law library and cursed, knowing he would need a student ID to get in. A young student came toward him, precariously balancing several books, and Whiskey saw his chance, the ID hanging loosely from his pocket.

The library was a spectacular building, and on another day, he might actually enjoy exploring it. At the desk, an older woman asked for his ID.

"Chan Yun Phat?" she questioned. He shrugged his shoulders.

"Adopted." She grinned but nodded in his direction. Whiskey wound his way through the bookshelves, not seeing who he was looking for. Spotting the staircase to the second level, he made his way up and started the same process of winding up and down the aisles. At the back of the stacks, he heard the noise too late as he was slammed into a rack of books. A fierce expression filled the face of Katarina Krevnyv as she reached up to hold a small knife at his throat.

"Tell my fucking father I don't need babysitters," she growled. Whiskey could only smile at the fierceness of the little lion. He had to give her credit. He outweighed her easily by a hundred pounds and had a good ten inches of height on her.

"I don't work for Daddy," he said, grinning. She shoved her forearm harder against his chest, but he could see the uncertainty in her face.

Oh hell! I am seriously outmanned with this guy, thought Kat. I can feel his muscles flexing below my arm like he's going to pounce. What the hell have I done?

"I want to speak with you about your father and his... business dealings," he said.

"I have *nothing* to do with my father and his business dealings," she practically spit the words at him.

"I believe you, beautiful. I just want to ask you some questions." She eyed him carefully up and down, looking around to see if there was anyone else. "You and I both know I could overpower you at any time. I'm not because I don't want to scare you or hurt you. I just want to talk to you."

Katarina seemed to be taking him in at that moment. He was so tall and muscular, his golden-brown eyes matching his hair, the sexy whiskers telling her he was no college student. This was a man, a man easily ten years her senior, if not more. She lowered the small knife and took a step back.

Whiskey then got a good view of what had been under that jacket. She wore an ivory sweater, clinging to small curves and a long torso. Her nearly white-blonde hair and blue eyes were the most beautiful combination he'd ever seen on a woman. He knew she was early twenties, but something in her eyes said she was much older.

"What do you want? Who are you?" she finally asked.

"Can we sit?" he asked.

"No." He grinned at her.

"Okay, my name is Wade English, but my friends call me Whiskey. I belong to a motorcycle club called the Steel Patriots. We help local and federal agencies find missing people, especially missing children and trafficked women."

He saw the hitch in her breath and the flicker of fear in her eyes. He started to reach for her, but she backed up, shaking her head.

"I don't know anything. Please leave me alone."

"Katarina, you may know more than you think you do. These girls… these children need our help. We think your father is holding them somewhere, and we need to find them. Now you're either helping us or helping your father. Which is it?"

"You know nothing of me!" she said, stabbing his chest with her finger. "I'm not helping my father. I want nothing to do with him. He's a monster!"

"Yes, he is," he said quietly. "With friends like Omar, he couldn't be classified as anything but a monster." Katarina sucked in a breath. How did he know about this? How could he know?

"I won't go. He can't make me…"

"You know that he can. He'll find a way, Kat. My men and I will protect you if you'll let us."

"Don't call me Kat; it's Katarina. I… you… you can't protect me, don't you understand? No one can protect me. As long as I'm here at school, he won't come for me." Whiskey shook his head and reached for her hand. The long delicate fingers linked with his own.

For just a moment, just a fraction of a moment, Katarina felt safe… felt hope fill her chest and then realized how foolish she was.

"If you let us, we can protect you. He can get to you anywhere, Kat. You know he can. He's already killed several young girls, and there are at last a dozen more out there somewhere in a truck waiting for him to deliver them to their deaths. Don't do this. Don't help him." Tears trailed down her alabaster cheeks, and she shook her head.

"I don't know anything. I don't live with him anymore, and I refuse to be involved in his activities. He's heinous, absolutely heinous. The FBI was supposed to get him out of the country after I helped them with my mother and brother. They lied! They lied to me, and now I have to tolerate his weekly dinners and visits. I have to hear him threaten me with... with Omar, and I won't. I refuse! I'll kill myself before I allow that man to lay a finger on me. I swear I will!"

"I believe you, beautiful," he said, letting out a long breath. "Listen, Katarina, I know you don't know me, but you can trust me. I promise you, I'm one of the good guys. I know you don't have a reason to believe that right now, but I want you to trust me when I say I won't let your father or Omar get to you if you'll just come with me, and let us help you."

She shook her head, biting that lower lip.

"Who... who are you really?" she asked.

"I told you who I really am. I'm Wade 'Whiskey' English. I'm retired United States Marine Corps, MARSOC sniper. I'm currently part of the Steel Patriots motorcycle club. Ask anyone except your father," he grinned, "and they'll tell you about us. We're legitimate, Katarina."

"Why... why would you help me?" she asked. Why indeed, thought Whiskey.

"Because I'm an idiot who can't refuse to help a beautiful woman."

CHAPTER THIRTY-THREE

Ace waited at the table in the interrogation room. Ed Stewart was awaiting a bail hearing, which he would damned sure make every attempt to stop. He'd been placed in general lock-up, much to his dismay, but to the great happiness of many of his fellow inmates. Even among thieves, there is a code, and molestation of children is not something they tolerate well.

The door opened, and the guard chained Stewart to the table, leaving as Ace nodded at him.

"Who are you? Are you my new lawyer?" asked Stewart.

"Not in this lifetime," said Ace. "I'm your worst fucking nightmare. Now, I'm going to ask you a few questions, and you're going to answer me or I'm going to make sure your friends in the cell block know every sick thing you've done." He jutted his dimpled chin defiantly.

"I've done nothing wrong!"

"Nothing? Luring twelve and thirteen-year-old girls to parties to dance and strip for men, be molested and raped, feed them drugs and alcohol, that's nothing?" Stewart paled and swallowed hard.

"I... I didn't do that!"

"Dude, you are wasting my fucking time. You have five seconds before I start beating the shit out of you."

"No, no, the guard..."

"The guard is an old Navy buddy. Owes me a favor. The girls..." he repeated.

Stewart looked back toward the door, not seeing a guard in sight. He swallowed again, his heart beating through his chest. He looked at the man across the table from him. His arms were covered in tattoos, his thick beard falling below his neck. He was heavily muscled with piercings visible on his body.

"I... I just got the girls to the party, man. That's all."

"That's all? So, you didn't ask the girls to dance? To strip?" Stewart looked away, his lips trembling. Ace wanted to punch him in the throat.

"Look, the girls were always hanging around me at school, flirting. I mean, have you seen the way some of these girls look at twelve and thirteen?" Ace gave him a death glare, and he swallowed hard once more. "I met Mabel a few years ago when she came to the school to speak about teenage runaways. We hit it off. She was raking in cash hand over fist. She said all I had to do was bring the girls to a party for a little inspection."

"What kind of party?" asked Ace.

"I put out some food, beer, and wine, and asked the girls to dance for the 'old guys.' Told them we were wanting to see the new moves. Shit, some of these girls danced like they were pole-trained," he grinned.

"Watch your fucking mouth," growled Ace.

"Right, well, most would dance, but some, well, when Mabel asked that we get them to show their bodies, some didn't want anything to do with it. They'd leave almost right away. Others... others were more than happy to strip for the old guys. Fuckers would have hard-ons the minute the girls started dancing."

"Then what?" Ace could barely speak through his clenched teeth.

"If the girls would let them touch them, we'd give them five hundred bucks, just touch their breasts or legs. If they let them put their hands between their legs, feel their pussies, they'd get another five hundred. Mabel wanted us to see how many of the girls were virgins.

The guys would just check. Shocked as shit how many weren't virgins, though, gotta tell ya."

"If they weren't virgins, some of the guys would offer the girls more money for blow jobs or to fuck. A few of them took it, not all."

"Who were the men?" asked Ace.

"I don't know." Ace slammed his fist against the table, the rattling of the chains clinking in the silence.

"Who... were... the... men?"

"I didn't know, not ever. Mabel would tell me how many were going to show and that was it. Some were foreign, some American, but I never knew who was showing up." Ace was seething with anger, and if he thought he could get away with it, he'd kill the little fucker right here.

"Alicia, tell me about her." Stewart smiled at Ace, but that only prompted Ace to reach for the man's throat.

"Whoa, whoa, I just, look, Alicia was a good kid. Her cousin was a drug-addled piece of shit who tried to rape her. She came to me, told me what happened because she was late on a paper. We got talking and she admitted to me that up until he tried to stick his dick all the way in, she liked it, liked what he was doing."

"And I suppose you offered to show her how it was done, right?" Ace was filled with disgust and loathing for the man. A child, he'd preyed on a child and her insecurities.

"I mean, yea, I told her it was about experience, and when done right, it felt good. Her mom couldn't make her rent, and Alicia was crying about it. I gave her eight hundred bucks and asked her to come to the party. She stripped right away. Man, she had huge tits for a twelve-year-old. I mean, the guys all wanted a piece of that." He looked up at the nearly purple face of Ace and turned away.

"She... she stripped, and then let the men touch her. She was still a virgin, but she enjoyed the attention a bit too much, if you ask me. Some Hispanic guy offered a grand to give him a blow job, and she dropped to her knees right away. Two nights later, she came to another party and sucked the guy off again while his buddy fucked her ass."

"You let these men do this to a twelve-year-old girl?"

"Look, man, she wanted it, okay? She was more than willing, and she was making some good money. Mabel wanted her for the auctions. I tried to convince her to let her stay. Her doing all that shit made the other girls curious. Mabel wouldn't hear of it. When I told Alicia she needed to go on a trip, she flipped out… wanted me with her."

"Then what?" Stewart looked at him like that was the stupidest fucking question in the world.

"Then she took her. Took her and a few other girls I had primed and said they wouldn't be back. End of discussion. I was on to the next batch."

"The next batch? The next batch, you prick? That girl was murdered. Brutally fucking raped, beaten, cut, and left for dead in the freezing cold. Other girls were found in a truck, dead, beaten, raped. You are responsible for that girl's death. You." Ace stood, folding up his laptop and shoving it in the leather backpack.

"You will never see the light of day. You will never touch another girl, and if I have my way, you will get the chair, and I will happily flip the switch on your ass, you filthy, disgusting piece of shit!" Stewart watched the man as he stood to leave.

"They were just a bunch of fucking cock-teasing girls, man. Just a bunch of…" He never got to finish his sentence as the fist of Alex "Ace" Mills, layered with thick silver rings, slammed into his face, silencing him.

Alex knocked on the door, and the guard opened it. Looking around his big body, he saw the prone body of Ed Stewart.

"Hit his head?" asked the guard.

"Yea, man, fainted and slammed his face into the table. Craziest shit I've ever seen," he grinned. The guard nodded.

"Heard everything, brother," he said soberly. "Fucker won't last long in here."

"Good, save the taxpayers a few dollars."

Ace hurried down the hallways desperate for fresh air, desperate to be out of reach of the vile creature he'd left in the interrogation room. As he stepped into the cold air, he spotted Whiskey on the steps waiting patiently. His friend looked up at him, concern filling his face.

"You okay, brother?" he asked. Ace shook his head. No, no, he would never be okay after that. Never.

"Will she talk to us? Katarina?" Whiskey shook his head as well.

"Isn't this a fine fucking day? Oh for two."

CHAPTER THIRTY-FOUR

"I have the address of Stewart's house," said Ace. "Figured before we head back, we'll take a look and see if we can find anything." Whiskey nodded, his elbow bent against the door frame, cold glass against his skin. He rubbed his face furiously.

"Katarina was scared. I mean, seriously scared, especially when I mentioned Omar," said Whiskey. "Said the feds were supposed to get Daddy out of the country after she helped with her mom and brother, but they never did."

"You think she might change her mind?" asked Ace.

"I don't know, man. She sure as shit doesn't trust anyone right now. I tried to make her feel comfortable with me. Little lioness pulled a knife on me," he grinned. Ace laughed at the thought of Whiskey getting caught off guard by a woman.

"What about Stewart?" he asked. Ace shook his head, quiet for the longest time.

"Fucking unbelievable, man. He led those girls to those parties knowing what he was doing. Let those men touch them, finger them, fuck them. Hell, they were giving blow jobs for cash. He was training them, priming them for sale. He and Mabel had a deal. He'd get the girls to the parties, and she'd cut him a percentage of the profits."

"Christ!" said Whiskey, rubbing his hands over his face. "What sort of fucked up world do we live in where people think that shit is okay?" Ace just shook his head. They fell silent again, neither needing to say anything to the other.

As they pulled in front of the small bungalow in Falls Church, Whiskey looked at Ace and back at the house.

"This is it?" he asked.

"Yep, this is his address," said Ace, stepping from the truck. They pulled the crime scene tape from the door, and with one good shove, the door gave way. Inside was a small open space, one sofa and a chair. The small kitchen only had barstools, no table and chairs. Down the hall were two small bedrooms and a bathroom.

"This can't be it," said Whiskey, frowning. "Neighbors up your ass here. You'd hear everything, see everything."

"I agree. Something isn't right." They searched what was left of the papers on the desk, and Ace started toward the back once more. Stepping into the hallway, the wood floorboards creaked beneath his heavy footsteps. He stepped forward and then back again, kneeling to press on the board.

Retrieving his pocketknife, he carefully slid the blade along the seam of the board and lifted.

"Jackpot," said Ace. Inside the floor were several bags of pills and cash along with a large envelope of photos and tapes.

"Fucker filmed the girls," said Whiskey. Ace nodded.

"Looks that way. Mabel probably didn't know. My guess is he was either going to blackmail her or sell the shit online." Whiskey continued down the hallway to be sure there wasn't another hiding space. Not finding anything, they went back to the truck.

"I'll get all this to my contact at the bureau," said Ace. Whiskey nodded, staring at the house and the neighborhood.

"This isn't where the parties happened, brother. I just know it. The house is too small, the neighbors too close. No one would be okay showing up here when teenage girls were seen going inside. I mean, think about it. I'm a forty-something-year-old dude with two other men my age. The neighbor sees me going into the house, and a little while later, a handful of pre-teen girls enter. You gonna tell me someone isn't gonna get suspicious and call the cops?"

"Yea," said Ace, looking around the neighborhood, "I definitely agree. There's another house. Looks like we're going back into the city."

CHAPTER THIRTY-FIVE

"Hello."

"Do you have the package?" asked Anton.

"I do. It's all tucked in nice and cozy." Mabel looked at the faces of the girls, all locked to the long bar at the table. She trusted only Silas in helping her now. The old man who'd run the convenience store was the last of the originals who could help. He guarded the girls. Their bodies were thin and weak from lack of food and water.

In front of them was one cup of water, three crackers, and a small bowl of chicken broth. They ate suspiciously, but most were so hungry, they didn't care where it came from or what was in it.

"Good, I can't get to you right now. I have some things I have to take care of, but I'll meet you at the farm in three days' time." Mabel only grinned into the phone. Anton was nervous. That was good in her book. That meant that if something happened to him, she would be totally in control. She wasn't stupid enough to kill him, but she would definitely take over when his ass was taken off to jail.

"When can I expect payment?" she asked. "I want an additional twenty thousand for having to house and feed the girls."

"Twenty thousand?" he ground out. "You'll get what we agreed upon. No more." He slammed the phone down and looked at the men around the room. Five bodyguards, whom he trusted not only with his life, but the life of his own daughter on occasion. A daughter, who at the moment was worth one million dollars to him.

He stood, moving toward the bookshelf, and stared at the photos of his wife and son, now gone. He couldn't prove it, but he was certain Katarina had something to do with their deaths. The FBI and Homeland went after them for selling children. After all, when these little sluts they sold got pregnant, something had to be done with the children. His beautiful wife, Ava, and their son, Sergei, came up with the idea to sell the children on the black market. So many unfortunate parents who couldn't have children of their own.

One evening while making a hand-off of a child, the FBI broke into the hotel and began shooting. They killed his family and the potential adopting family. No one apologized. No one said where the information had come from. Now he was alone with a daughter who despised him, and a business that was crumbling beneath him if he didn't do something quickly.

"Where is my daughter?" asked Anton.

"She should be in her townhome, sir." Anton nodded, looking out the big window of the estate once again.

"Bring her to me."

CHAPTER THIRTY-SIX

It was nearly ten by the time Ace and Whiskey walked back into the club. Ghost immediately called a meeting with the two of them, Doc, Tango, Gunner, and Zulu. They listened intently as Ace walked them through the conversation he'd had with Stewart.

Several times, one or more of the men would stand, pacing the room as if caged. The anger and rage filling their bodies would fuel their energy to hunt down Mabel and Anton.

"We went back to the jail," said Ace. "By the time I arrived, he'd already met his maker in the yard. Someone severed his spine, left him bleeding beneath some bleachers. I have no clue now where the fuck the other house was."

"It's not your fault, Ace," said Ghost. "We couldn't have known there would be two houses. We'll just have to keep digging. What about Katarina?"

"She refused our help. She said she's not helping her old man, but she doesn't want anything to do with us or him. She's scared, that much was for sure, knew the name Omar when I said it, and it damned sure showed on her face."

"Does she understand how much danger she's in?" asked Ghost.

"She seems to, but I just couldn't convince her to come with me. I mean, for fuck's sake, she's not much more than a kid herself."

"Brother, that woman is almost twenty-three years old. She's a full-grown woman. She's been a principal dancer with the D.C. ballet, a dean's list student at Georgetown, and now she's in law school. My guess is, in her lifetime, she's seen more sickness and deranged behavior than any woman twice her age. She might be scared, but she's no fucking kid," said Tango. Whiskey nodded at his friend. He knew that what he said was true, but it didn't change Whiskey's protective instincts over the young girl.

"CMP says they think Mabel crossed the border six days ago. Drones caught a woman and two men walking through northern New York, disappearing somewhere in Buffalo. She fit the description. She was seen again near Philadelphia by a street camera."

"She's headed this way," said Ace. "If she's been on video camera, I can try and track her path to figure out where she went. It will take me a while. There are a million fucking possibilities, but I'll bet I can find her given time."

"Problem is we don't have a lot of time, brother," said Doc. "Those poor girls don't have a lot of time." Ace nodded, standing to head to his computer room.

"Ace? I know you're doing everything you can," said Doc apologetically. Ace gave him a quick head shake and left the room.

"I know you weren't in the room when he spoke to Stewart, but any indication of where this other place might be, or who the men were who visited?" asked Doc.

"No on the other house. As far as the men, he told Ace they were mostly foreigners, a few Americans. They didn't force the girls but lured them with money. They definitely checked them for virginity. My guess is, if they were virgins, they got a higher price for them." Ghost and Doc nodded.

"His purchases," said Tango. All eyes turned toward him. "the alcohol and food for the parties. We could track the purchases and see where he was buying the food and beverage. If it was close to his house, then we're nowhere, but..."

"... but if it's somewhere else..." said Doc, smiling.

"Get on it," said Ghost. "Let's catch these people and save those girls."

CHAPTER THIRTY-SEVEN

Doc locked the door to Bree's rented cottage and closed the blinds, taking a deep cleansing breath, relieving his body of thoughts of work and children in danger. He kicked off his shoes at the door and laid his keys in the bowl on the table. Making his way down the hall, he saw the small bedside lamp on and frowned.

Since returning from Toronto, she'd slept with a light on almost every night. It didn't bother Doc much, but he knew that she was most likely having nightmares or seeing things in the dark that was preventing her from sleeping well.

He pulled his sweatshirt over his head and unbuckled his jeans, shoving them to his ankles. He slid between the sheets, careful not to move too much and wake her. Her body seemed to sense his own, and she rolled toward him feeling the heat of his skin against her own. Doc kissed the top of her head and felt her leg lift up and over his hip.

Rubbing his big palm over her thigh, curving to that perfectly round ass, he could feel himself harden. He didn't want it to happen. He wanted her to sleep, but damned if his dick didn't have other thoughts. She moaned and grabbed his hand, bringing it to her breast, she squeezed her hand over his, squeezing her breast. She guided his fingers to her nipples, and he happily obliged, pinching one between his thumb and forefinger.

"I'm so glad you're back," she moaned. He laughed.

"I can see that," he said, kissing her. She rolled over and took him with her, his body now pressed against her soft flesh. He squeezed her breasts again, sucking on one nipple and then another. "Have I mentioned how much I love your fucking tits?"

"I believe you have," she smiled. "But since you brought it up, why don't you do just that, fuck my tits." Doc groaned, grinding against her thigh. He knelt above her, placing his legs on either side of her chest.

"You sure, baby?" he asked. She nodded, biting her lower lip. Reaching inside the bedside table, he found a small bottle of baby oil and squirted some on her breasts. Just the shiny, glistening effect of the oil on those milky white breasts made his dick rock hard.

Bree smiled up at him gripping her breasts and squeezing them together. Doc laid his cock between her huge mounds of flesh, the big red nipples erect, begging to be played with, he started moving back and forth.

"Oh, fuck, baby, fucking hell!" he cried. She loved knowing that she had him in her control, his pleasure was hers to own as she squeezed the fleshy globes around his hard rigid mass. The tip poking in and out, she lowered her chin and licked at him every time he came near her mouth.

Doc gripped her hair, driving harder and harder toward her face. He was going to blow all over that beautiful face if she wasn't careful.

"Fuck... Bree... baby..."

"Do it!" she called. "I want to taste you. Do it, cum all over me..." Doc let out a loud yell, the hot liquid of his desire spraying all over her beautiful face, neck and chest. The thick creamy sex seemingly endless. Bree smiled at him, taking a finger and swiping at the big drops on her chin, licking each one as she did. Doc groaned, gliding down her body.

"My turn," he moaned. He pushed her knees apart and opened her wide, sliding a finger down her wet, warm cunt. He flicked his tongue out, tasting her sex, and he was hard again. Placing her feet on his shoulders, he shoved her hips higher, tongue in and out of her pussy.

"Oh... ohhh yea... Jack... Jack, that's it, baby..." He wet his finger and let it glide down the crack of her ass until he found the tight hole he wanted, sliding the finger inside. She squeezed, and he slapped her ass cheek. Giggling, she relaxed as he continued to dive in and out of her pussy.

"Fuck, you taste so good," he moaned against her. His hot breath made her even hotter. Doc let another finger slip into her tight hole, and he moaned with desire, the ache in his cock overwhelming. The need so great, he shoved his tongue in further, working her ass with his fingers.

"Yes... oh fuck... yes... that's it..." she cried as her release squirted all over his face. Bree shook with satisfaction as he lapped up her juices. Doc gripped her hips and flipped her over.

"I need this ass, baby," he said, shoving her shoulders to the mattress. She only nodded, looking back at him with a trusting expression. He grabbed the oil and spread a light film over her tight hole. Touching the tip of the big mushroom head to her ass, he groaned from a painful need.

"Oh God... yes... Jack, I need this, baby..." she cried. He let himself fall into her a little at a time until he was completely seated in her ass, his heavy balls feeling the wet pussy. He stilled, knowing that he would not last long like this.

"Move, Jack… for fuck's sake… please…" He grinned at her and started to move.

"Touch yourself, baby… play with that beautiful clit." She groaned, her ass moving back and forth against him, fingering her already sensitive little bud.

"Harder, Jack… harder… I know you want to…" With one hand gripping a fistful of hair and the other slapping her ass, he drove into her over and over again. He could feel her fingers playing with her clit, but when she let her own hand glide inside her pussy, he fucking lost it, slamming against the big white ass cheeks.

"Ahhhh…" he growled.

"Yes! That's it… Jack, I'm cumming again… oh…" she howled with satisfaction as he pulled back on her hair again, ramming her so hard he thought he might have hurt her. His cock emptied into her tight little ass, the river of juice falling from her as he pulled out, completely spent. She rolled to look up at him, a smile of satisfaction on her face.

"That was amazing," she said, grinning at him.

"Yea," he said breathlessly, "it damned sure was. What brought all that on?" She shrugged her shoulders as she scooted closer to him.

"I just needed you. Needed to feel you. I'll never be able to thank you all for everything you've done, Jack. Never. Finding the girls, finding Alicia, it was more than you could imagine." He nodded, kissing her temple.

"You don't have to thank me, baby. This is what we do." She hugged him tightly, her tongue gliding along his lips, kissing, nibbling. "You wanna shower?"

"Nope," she said, grinning. "I want to go to sleep drowning in our love, in your love. I want to wake up and feel your cum," she kissed him, "dripping from my ass, my pussy, my mouth…" she said each word in a breathless whisper and fuck him if he wasn't hard again.

"Fucking hell, woman," he said, covering her body with his own. His cock was hard again, sliding between her creamy thighs. "Now, look what you've done."

"What a shame," she said, pulling him down for a passionate kiss. "Fuck me again, Jack. Fuck me until that beautiful cock of yours is worn out. I need you, baby."

What the hell was happening with his woman? She was fucking hot as hell tonight, and he damned sure wasn't going to complain about it. His cock was loving the dirty talk. Pounding into her tight, wet pussy he smiled as he glanced at the nightstand and her latest romance novel. He couldn't help but send up a silent thank you to the author.

Whoever the fuck you are, thank you, and keep writing that shit!

CHAPTER THIRTY-EIGHT

The girls all looked at one another, their faces filled with a myriad of emotions – fear, hunger, confusion, panic, sadness. They'd been gone for weeks now, cold, hungry and hurting. Barely having a moment alone to talk to one another, they didn't even know their names. They knew that the youngest was ten, the oldest was fourteen, but that's all.

"We have to run," said one of the girls.

"How can we do that? We're chained to one another and this wall," said the youngest girl. "I want to go home. I want my mom and dad."

"I know you do," said the older girl sitting next to her. "We all do. I... I'm from Texas. Where are you guys from?" They looked at one another, almost afraid to answer at first.

"Missouri," said one. Two more nodded.

"Florida," said another girl, three nodded at that.

"Louisiana," said the youngest girl.

The fourteen-year-old girl nodded at her, smiling. It had all been so innocent. She'd gone to a party with a boy she knew through a girlfriend. It was supposed to be high school boys, but she knew immediately these guys weren't in high school. They weren't even in college. They were much older. She should have listened to her instincts and run from that party. She should have never spoken to that girlfriend again, left her there.

At first, they just asked the girls to dance, and she thought it was funny that they wanted to see a bunch of little girls dance. Eleven years of dance made her limber, and she showed the other girls her spins and ballet moves. The men seemed to enjoy it, and then she saw their pants tented, and she knew.

Living with her dad and two brothers, she knew what that meant. She'd walked in on her brother once while he was rubbing his penis while looking at a magazine. Hiding behind the door, she watched the stuff shoot from the tip of his penis and thought it was disgusting, but she was also curious.

At first, she thought it was funny, but the next day she looked through a biology book in the library and figured out what it was, and it wasn't funny anymore. A few more times while watching movies, she would notice her brothers with their pants tented. When she looked their way, they would put a pillow over their laps, flushing in embarrassment. She knew what those men wanted, and it was sick.

One of them made her sit on his lap, and he rubbed his hands between her thighs. Panicking, she leapt from his lap and went back to dance with her friends. He'd laughed, nodding at the others, and she could only pray the night would end soon.

Leaving the party, she and her friends headed back home. The next day, the same guy who invited her to the party asked her to go to a movie with him and him alone. She agreed but said she didn't want to ever go to a party like that again. She should have said no. She'd kissed her dad goodbye and waved at her brothers, who made kissy faces at her.

They never got to the movies. Drugged and completely out of it, she woke up in the back of that trailer with the other girls, terrified, alone, and only wanting her father.

"It's just one old man and old woman," she said. "Maybe when he comes down here next, we can jump him."

"We don't have shoes," said one of the girls. "It's cold outside. We'll die."

"We might die in here. We have to try and find someone to help us," she said. The younger girl started to cry, and she pulled her close. "I'm sorry, I didn't mean to scare you, but we can't just sit here and do nothing."

"I'm tired," said one of the other girls. The others nodded, lying on the cold hard basement floor. They'd each been given one blanket, no pillows. There was a bucket in the corner to go to the bathroom, but that was the extent of their comforts. Nothing more.

"Get some sleep. We'll talk more tomorrow," she whispered. Across the room, one of the other girls looked at her and nodded. They needed to get out of there, and they needed to do it soon. She stood, stretching the chains as far as she could. Two boxes in the corner were within her grasp, and she pulled them to her. Socks. Mismatched socks. Of all the stupid things to keep in a box in the basement. The other contained some old tools that she had no idea how to use.

Help me, Dad... if you can hear me... help me.

If the old woman came back again, she would probably shoot them. She'd wielded the gun in their faces on more than one occasion.

But the old man was usually alone, and he didn't appear to have a weapon. If they could get the jump on him, they might have a chance.

I only need one chance.

CHAPTER THIRTY-NINE

Seated around the table, the team reviewed the data once more.

"So, he bought some things near his home, but most of the stuff was bought further out near the more rural communities?" asked Doc, staring at Ace and Tango.

"Looks that way. He'd buy liquor close to his house. My guess is because he could store that in his car, and it wouldn't go bad. If you look at the date stamps, he'd buy it late at night or early in the morning like maybe before he went to work." Tango spread the copies of the credit card receipts, pointing to the purchases.

"Okay, so the food was bought at one of seven small grocery stores on the outskirts," said Doc. "That's where this other house is going to be. I think when Alicia kept saying 'the falls,' she might have been trying to tell me the Falls Church area."

"That's a fuck lot of territory, Doc," said Whiskey. "I mean, that's high dollar property out there. Folks aren't likely to just open their doors to a bunch of us and say, 'yea come on in, grungy biker dudes.' They'll be suspicious of us."

"They won't be suspicious of us," came the voice behind them. Standing in the doorway were Bree and Grace.

"Oh, fuck no!" yelled Ghost. "You will get your pregnant ass back to the house and wait."

"Ghost, Eric," she said, cupping his jaw. "If this were our children, wouldn't you want someone, anyone to care enough to be out there?" He grimaced, folding his arms over his chest, staring at his beautiful fiancée.

"I'm going, Jack," said Bree. "Whether you like it or not, I'm going. I can help with those girls when they're found, and they will be found. But more importantly, people are more likely to speak with us."

"I hate this idea," said Ace, "but they're right. People will more likely speak with them than anyone else. People are sympathetic to women and children, and with Grace being pregnant, they'll be more so."

"Shut the fuck up," growled Ghost.

"You know he's right, brother," said Whiskey, staring at the two women. "Do you both know how to shoot?"

"You know I do," said Grace, smiling. "Between the twins and Ghost, I'm pretty good." Ghost rolled his eyes, shoving his hand through his hair.

"I know how to shoot," said Bree. "But you said something that made me think. The twins." Both men looked at her, their eyes huge.

"What about us?" they said in unison.

"They look like college kids if you shave the beards off. Put them in button-down shirts, blazers, and fix their hair. They look like they belong out in those big fancy houses, kids home for college or something. We take them, and we'll have protection and handsome young faces to help with this."

"What the fuck is wrong with our hair?" asked Eagle.

"That's what you picked up in that?" yelled Doc. "They want to pimp your asses to lonely suburban housewives, you idiot."

"No, no, that's not - well, not exactly," smiled Bree. Grace laughed, seeing the faces of the men in the room.

"Listen," said Grace, "Bree is right. Housewives will immediately be drawn to them. Older women might be more drawn to Bree and me. Together I think we can ask some questions that might get us somewhere.

Give us a photo of Stewart and Mabel, and let's see if we find out some information."

"I don't like this," said Doc, staring at Ghost.

"I don't either, but we're running out of options and time for those girls." Just as Ghost was ready to speak again, the phone rang, Ivan's number popping up. He stared at the women who stood, arms folded, challenging him.

"Fuck!" He pressed the speaker button. "Ivan, what's up, brother?"

"I still don't know where the girls are, but they're going to move them in three days. That's all I know for now. I'll try to get more information, but he's keeping this one tight-lipped. He knows the feds are wanting to talk to him, and Mabel has gone to ground."

"Thanks, brother," said Ghost. The line went dead, and he looked up at the two women. "Alright. Eagle and Hawk? One scratch to either of them, and I'll kill you both myself." The men nodded. They might be juvenile delinquents around the club, but they took the safety of the women seriously, and more than that, they understood the ramifications of not completing this job.

"Alright," said Doc. "Let's take a drive."

CHAPTER FORTY

"So, we go into each of the stores on this list and just ask the check-out girls, managers, anyone, if they've seen either of them. Then get out," said Hawk. "Understand?" Both women nodded, and he waited patiently.

"Understand," said Grace, smiling.

"Understand," said Bree, mimicking her friend. "You look handsome, by the way." He blushed and shook his head. He damned sure wasn't going to risk getting his ass kicked by acknowledging that compliment. He'd done what they thought was best by wearing khakis, button-down shirt, a blazer, and dress shoes, which right now were hurting the fuck out of his feet.

Stepping inside the upscale market, the women made their way around the aisles, moving back toward the bakery where they knew many items were purchased.

"Can I help you, ladies?" asked the man behind the counter.

"Yes," said Bree, "I hope so. A friend of mine recently catered a party and had the most scrumptious little tea cakes. I think he said he got them here. His name is Ed Stewart. This is his photo, if that helps." The man eyed Bree looking down at the photo. He'd been asked weird shit before but remembering an order by the photo of the person who ordered it? That was top of the list.

"I don't know, lady. I get a lot of people in here. What was it he ordered? Something special?" he asked.

"Oh, tea cakes is all I know, maybe Russian tea cakes," Bree said without thinking.

"Hmmm, okay, that rings a bell with me," he said, staring at the women. "Younger guy used to come in here and order tons of sweets trays. You'd think he was throwing kids' parties with all those sweets." Neither woman said a thing as he thumbed through the order book.

"Here it is. Last order was more than a month ago. Tea cakes, cookies, empanadas, of all the weird things. I think he had a big deli order as well."

"Did he pick it up, or did you deliver it?" asked Grace.

"What does that have to do with what he ordered?" asked the man suspiciously. Shit! Grace cursed under her breath.

"Nothing," said Bree. "We were just hoping you offered delivery. I mean, with my friend here being pregnant, we really can't carry a lot ourselves."

He eyed both women and nodded, looking back at the orders.

"He picked everything up. We offer some delivery options, but either he wanted to pick it up himself, or it was too far out. Either way, I think I've helped you enough, ladies." The man closed the book and turned his back on the women. Bree let out a breath and looked over at Grace.

"Well, it was something. If he didn't order from here in over a month, he had to have ordered from somewhere else in the last month because that party Alicia attended was within the last month." Grace nodded at Bree as they made their way outside. Hawk and Eagle were standing at the truck waiting patiently.

"Anything?" asked Eagle. Grace and Bree told them everything the man at the bakery had given them. It wasn't much, but it was more than they had a few hours ago.

"Same for us. The manager remembered seeing Stewart a few times because his orders were so large, they would help him to the car with them. Said he was always friendly, tipped the baggers well. Told us just what you said. He hasn't been in here in over a month."

"Well, it's late now. I guess we come back tomorrow?" Eagle nodded at Bree, leading the women to the truck. Another day those poor girls were lost. Another day their parents were filled with fear and concern.

Hang on, little ones, we're coming.

CHAPTER FORTY-ONE

Mabel had every intention of going out to the farmhouse tonight, but best-laid plans and all that shit. She watched from outside the residence of Anton Krevnyv and smiled. Something was definitely going on. Men had been scurrying in and out all day.

The bastard was not going to deny her this last shipment. She needed this one final payout. In her head, there had always been a number that would equal retirement and freedom. She was nearly there. The girls at the farm were unharmed, for the most part, and prime. Her partners all over the country came through with this shipment. Anton was not going to screw with her.

A long black town car pulled in front of the house, and she watched as a tall, thin man with a long beard stepped from the car. He was dressed in traditional Arab garb. There was an air of superiority to him that Mabel recognized immediately.

"Asshole is trying to do business without me," she mumbled.

The Arab went inside the house with his entourage, and several moments later, a silver Mercedes pulled into the driveway. Stepping from the car was one of Anton's favorite bodyguards, Alexei. A young woman with long blonde hair stepped from the car, her tight blue jeans and sweater showing off her definite assets.

She attempted to pull her arm free from Alexei's grip but to no avail. Mabel laughed at that. Yea, she wouldn't get away from him, that's for damned sure.

Almost twenty years of pinching pennies, wearing used clothing, buying day-old bread, fighting the bill collectors. Twenty years of listening to the misery of others, yet no one listened to her during her time of misery.

Oh, they'd come to that crappy apartment in Pittsburgh only to believe the bullshit lies spewing from her husband's mouth. Her nose would be broken, eyes black, mouth bloody and ripped open, and they would fall for the bullshit line of 'I fell down the stairs.' Every damned time.

She'd tried to run so many times. Tried to get help, and every time he pulled her back. Then she got smart. Tried to avoid him in anger. Give him what he wanted in bed, bide my time. Saving a few dollars here and there after groceries, she stashed the money aside waiting.

After visiting one of the neighbors one day, asking them to please turn down their music, she noticed a pistol laying on top of the stereo system. The guy was so wasted, he never even took notice of her. She took that pistol, tucked it behind the toilet, and waited.

He always projected when he was visiting a whore. He was excited, and it wasn't for Mabel. That night, he said he'd be out late watching the game with the guys. No idea what game but the game. She followed him to that cheap-ass motel. When she opened that door, and the whore was sucking him off, she lifted the pistol and killed him first and then the whore.

It took her hours to get him into the car, he was so much bigger than she was. Finally loaded in her trunk, she took off toward a remote railroad bridge over the Allegheny. Dragging him, his head beating against the rails over and over again, each time satisfaction filled her chest, she finally pushed his body over the edge, watching it sink into the murky waters.

Driving to Arlington was like freedom. It was fresh air and freedom. Finding that congressmen fucking that poor little girl was just luck. But Mabel never looked a gift horse in the mouth nor an opportunity, and there it was right in front of her. She'd invited that congressman in to chat, fucked him to his satisfaction, and made the deal.

Now the future was hers. She would be free of teenage girls, free of Anton, and free of fear. Finally, she was going to breathe in true freedom.

Something was happening at the house as men raced from the front door. The Arab was screaming at his driver, and Anton yelled at his men. Mabel looked across the vast expanse of green lawn and saw what they were seeking, a blonde running for her life.

CHAPTER FORTY-TWO

After visiting the next three stores on their list, the team had no luck in uncovering anything else that might lead to the whereabouts of the girls or Mabel. In the final store, speaking to the manager, he spotted the photo of Mabel and smiled.

"You didn't tell me you folks knew Mabel!" he smiled. "What a gem! Helping all those poor lost girls like she does. Just a wonderful woman."

"Yes," said Bree, biting back the bile and curses, "I was one of those lost girls she saved. Actually, I'm a bit worried for her. She usually calls me every week, and I haven't heard from her. You wouldn't happen to have her address out here, would you?"

"Well, if you were friends, wouldn't you know that?" he asked suspiciously.

"I've been to the farmhouse," said Bree. Okay, let those college theater classes come to life. "I mean, it's huge, right? Big front porch. I just don't remember the address." He nodded at her, smiling.

"That's it. Huge white front porch, green shutters. Pretty old place. Needs some fixing up, but well, Mabel on her own and all can't do everything. I actually don't really know the address myself, but I know that it's out off of Stallion Mile Road. Nothin' but beautiful horse farms out there."

"That's so helpful. I bet I can find it from there," she said, smiling at the man. "Thank you so much!"

Exiting the store, Eagle called Ghost.

"Brother, we have an area to cover, but according to the map, it's a lot. There must be sixty houses on that road."

"We're on our way," said Ghost. "Don't move from there. We'll take it in teams of three and see if we can get some luck between us."

Waiting for Ghost, Doc, Tango, Whiskey, and Zulu, they drank a cup of coffee in the shop next door. It was starting to snow, and Bree could feel the fear rising in her body. If those girls were out there in the cold, they wouldn't survive long in the weather.

"Shit, just what we need," said Eagle. "Fucking snow. It's going to make it hard to track anyone if they're on the run."

"We have to try," said Bree. The men nodded. An hour later, the trucks pulled in with the remainder of the team. They split into groups of three, with Bree, Doc, and Eagle in one; Ghost, Grace, and Zulu in another; and finally, Tango, Whiskey and Hawk in the last.

"Alright, old-fashioned knocking on the door, house to house," said Ghost. They followed one another, the GPS leading them to Stallion Mile Road. Turning onto the road, Ghost stopped.

"Fuck! Look at this shit. These houses are massive, and most of them are gated. This is going to take forever."

"Then let's get going!" yelled Grace. He turned and smiled at his woman, picking up his phone and calling the other two.

They took each house, asking for entrance based on looking for one lost little girl. Almost all of the homeowners allowed them in right away. Bree walked up the front steps of a huge ranch house and rang the doorbell.

"Hello, I called from the gate," she said to the woman at the door. She was probably in her early seventies, her clear gray eyes smiling up at her.

"Yes, dear, you said something about a lost child?"

"Yes, ma'am. These are my friends Jack and, ummm, Eagle?" Bree looked at Eagle, flushing a bright pink.

"Tyran, ma'am. I go by Tyran," he flashed his panty-melting smile at the older woman, and she giggled.

"Well, I wish I could help, but I haven't seen any lost children, dear."

"I see," said Bree. "Well, we think she might have been staying with a friend of mine, Mabel Beckstein."

"Oh, yes! Mabel's been a neighbor of ours for years now. Moved into that big old house probably ten years ago, although she doesn't come out here very much. That job of hers in the city keeps her so busy." Bree could feel the excitement filling her chest and sensed the anxiety of the two big men behind her.

"Yes, ma'am, it's been years since I was out here, and I guess I'm turned around. Can you point me back that way?" Bree smiled at the woman and her sparkling eyes laughed.

"Of course! Just follow the road to the end at the cul-de-sac. Her house is the only one there off the road." Bree reached out and hugged the woman.

"Thank you so much!" Doc stepped forward and handed the woman his card.

"Ma'am, we'd sure appreciate it if you'd call us if you see that little girl or her friends." The woman eyed him suspiciously and nodded. Stepping off the porch, he reached for his phone and shot a text to the other two vehicles.

"Let's go."

CHAPTER FORTY-THREE

"Does everyone understand?" said the girl. Their little heads nodded as they all took their seats, heads resting on their knees. They heard the basement door open, their little hearts beating through their chests.

"Wake up," said the old man. "Everyone up. We're going upstairs for breakfast, and it shouldn't be long, and you'll be out of here." Panic filled the girls, but they were going to trust the older girl from Texas. She had a plan, and if it worked, they would run.

He made his way to the big lock on the wall that released the chain. One of the girls moaned, writhing on the floor.

"What's the matter with her?" he asked.

"She's been sick all night, not sure," said the girl next to her.

"Damn! This is all I need right now," he said, kneeling over the girl. "What's the matter..." *Thwack!* The huge wrench made a sickening thud on the back of his head. He tilted forward against the wall. "Wh... what..." *Thwack! Thwack!*

Again and again, she hit him with the oversized wrench. He'd touched them all, he'd been a part of this, and she would make him pay, make sure he wouldn't rise from that cold floor.

"Stop!" yelled one of the girls. "Stop! He's dead. He's dead. You have blood... blood all over you now."

"I don't care," she said, breathing heavily.

"We have to go," said the little girl. She nodded, putting the wrench in her back pocket. Taking the box of socks, she handed them to each of the girls.

"Put one on each hand and two pairs on your feet. It won't be a lot, but it will help. We're going to run together." She searched the old man's pockets and found the keys. Each girl did as the older girl told her and then headed toward the stairs. She put a finger to her lips. Opening the basement door, she stepped out into the morning light of the kitchen.

Listening carefully, she waited. Waving the other girls up, she grabbed the loaf of bread on the counter and handed each one two pieces.

"Let's go. We eat as we run." At the front door, she saw cars moving up and down the street. Not sure if one might be the older woman, she looked out the back door and saw a house across the field. "There, that house. We'll run across the field to that house and ask them to call the police."

"How can we be sure it's safe?" asked the little girl.

"We can't, but if it's not, I still have the wrench," she said, pulling the tool from her back pocket.

Holding hands, the girls stepped into the frigid air of Virginia and ran across the field. It only took a few steps, and the socks were soaked through, their feet already cold, but what choice did they have?

"I'm c-cold," said the littlest one.

"I know. I know," she said. "Look, we're getting closer now. It's not that far. We can do it. We're going to be safe." She pushed the girls across the field, finally picking up the younger one and putting her on her back. Her feet were frozen solid now, and they hurt so bad she wanted to cry.

At the wide wooden fence of the house, she helped each of the girls over and then walked slowly to the front door ringing the doorbell.

"Oh, my."

CHAPTER FORTY-FOUR

"There!" said Bree. The men leapt from the SUVs, and Doc turned, looking at Bree.

"Stay right here, Bree. I'm not fucking around, sit your ass right here." She nodded, not happy but stayed. Looking into the other SUV, she spotted Grace and smiled, waving. Grace shrugged her shoulders and waved back.

Whiskey tried the door, looking up at the others to indicate it was unlocked. Weapons drawn, they used their usual pattern to clear each room. Doc waved at the men, nodding toward the basement door.

Ghost took lead, Doc behind him. Tango was at the top of the stairs waiting. The smell of urine and feces hit their noses, and they brought their shirts up over their nose and mouth to cover the odor.

"Chains," said Zulu. "And... dead body" Ghost shone the light on the now unrecognizable head. Blood, bone fragments, and brain matter splattered all over the basement walls. Doc knelt next to the body and felt the wrist and forearm.

"He's been dead less than a few hours, I'd say. Still pretty warm. Shit," said Doc. "You think the girls did this? They got away?"

"I don't know. Let's get upstairs and see if we can get some search parties out here. Check around the property. See if we can find any footprints. When the sun sets, it's going to be fucking cold out here, and they won't survive."

"Doc?" asked Hawk. "Look here, a box of socks strewn on the floor."

"Clever girls. If they didn't have shoes, they'd probably use those or put them on as mittens. They won't last long in them, but it's better than nothing."

"Let's get upstairs," said Ghost. Gathering around the SUVs, they told the girls what they found, and both felt hope spring in their chests. Doc hugged Bree, kissing her forehead as Ghost made the call back to the club. If he could get ten or twenty more men out, they might be able to track the girls down. Doc's phone rang, and he pulled it from his pocket.

"Hello?"

"Yes, is this the handsome young man who was here earlier with that pretty redheaded girl and the really handsome younger man?" asked the sweet voice. Doc smiled and winked at Bree.

"Yes, ma'am. Jack Harris, ma'am."

"Well, you asked me to call you if that little girl showed up." She sounded so sweet, and Doc could hear small voices in the background.

"Yes, ma'am," he said excitedly as he snapped his fingers to get everyone's attention. He placed the phone on speaker.

"Well, I didn't get one little girl, but ten little girls just showed up at my door all beat up and freezing. I'm feeding them now, but I think maybe you could help them."

"Yes, ma'am, we sure can. We're on our way. And ma'am?"

"Yes, son," she said sweetly.

"Lock your doors."

CHAPTER FORTY-FIVE

It was late afternoon by the time Mabel pulled up to the farmhouse. There were no lights on, and she cursed, wondering if that old fool, Silas, was sleeping already. Opening the door, she stepped into an eerily quiet house.

"Hello? Silas?" she yelled. "Fuck! I have to do everything myself." She flipped on the lights and moved toward the basement door. Walking down the steps, she turned the light on and immediately noticed that the girls were gone.

"No! No, no, this can't be happening!" She looked at the body of whom she knew was Silas and cursed, taking the steps as fast as her old legs could carry her. I have to get out of here. She hit the button on her phone and waited as the line rang, running toward her car.

She locked her car door and took off out of the driveway, driving as fast as she could.

"What?" yelled the Russian on the other end of the line.

"They're gone, Anton! The girls, they're all gone. Silas is dead in the basement, and the girls are gone." She was panicked.

"When?" he asked.

"How the hell do I know? He's been out here for two days by himself. It could have been any time during the last forty-eight hours. His head is bashed in, and the girls are nowhere to be found. I need some men to help us find them."

"No."

"What? Anton, we have to find those girls, or they will name us both in this." She pleaded, taking the entrance to the interstate. She had no idea where she would go, but she needed to be as far away from the house as possible.

"No, we don't need to get away. You do. They never saw me. They did, however, see you. You are the one they will identify, Mabel, not me."

"You fucking asshole, you piece of shit, I can incriminate you in this as well!" she yelled into the speaker. "If those girls name me, I will not be the only one going down. I can assure you of that."

"Do not threaten me, Mabel. I can bury you, and you know it. Leave the girls. Get out of the country, and don't come back. You had no clue who you were fucking with when you shot the boyfriend of the redhead, did you? He's a former Army Ranger. Now part of a do-gooder motorcycle club. He wasn't just anyone, and yet you treated him that way. A bullet in the leg? That was a flea bite to him. A bullet in the head is what he needed. You failed, not me. Take care, Mabel. Enjoy retirement. I have something urgent that needs my attention." The call ended, and she slammed her phone against the steering wheel, cracking the glass.

"Damn! Damn! Damn!" she yelled. The fucking bitch, Bree, and her boyfriend, it had to be them. What the hell was she going to do now? Get out of the country. Leave now while you still can. Leave!

"I'll leave," she whispered to herself. "Once I've killed them, once and for all."

CHAPTER FORTY-SIX

Doc watched as the girls ate the sandwiches the woman had put out for them. Their wary gazes traveled over his face and then toward the other men. They looked at Bree and Grace, then hovered over the food as if it would be stolen from them. Their faces were filthy, their hair dirty, clothes torn, but they were alive.

"Are they okay?" asked Ghost.

"All have some minor frostbite on their extremities, but other than dehydration and malnourishment, they're doing pretty well. I tried to get closer, but they're terrified of me," he said, wanting to cry. Those poor girls had no idea the lengths he would go to protect them.

"It's okay, brother," said Ghost. "We called social services, and they're on their way out with a bus. Sheriff is down at Mabel's place with Zulu now, waiting on the coroner. We got them, Doc. That's all that matters." He nodded at his friend as Bree chatted casually with the girls.

"Are you feeling okay?" she asked them. Their heads didn't move, just stared at her. It was the little one that finally cracked.

"My... my fingers hurt," she said, tears filling her eyes.

"I know, sweet girl," said Bree. "You know, these big men are good men. They've been searching for all of you, trying to find you. They would never in a million years hurt you. You know how I know?" Ten little heads shook in her direction.

"I know because he's my boyfriend. He's also a nurse and can help you. Will you let him?" Bree noticed the oldest girl looking at the others and nodded. She waved Doc over, who walked slowly, lowering himself carefully to the chair so as not to frighten the girls. Hawk and Eagle stepped up behind him.

"Are they twins?" asked the littlest girl. Eagle and Hawk both flashed big smiles. Their youthful, handsome faces eased some of the fear for the girls.

"I told you she was smart and pretty," said Eagle, nudging his twin. "We are twins, little one. What's your name?"

"Amanda. Are you going to take me home to my mom and dad?" she said with a quivering lip.

"We are, honey. I promise we are." Eagle scooted closer to her, and she started eating once again.

Doc looked at the hands of the oldest girl, who seemed the worst. Her feet definitely had frostbite, but he didn't think she would lose any toes. She winced as he looked at the hands.

"I'm sorry," he said softly.

"It's okay. It's not a big deal," she said, trying to be brave. He noticed the blood caked on her hands and around her face. She'd been the brave one.

"She gave us her socks," said one of the other girls. "We were cold, and she gave us her socks. It was still cold, but it was better for a while." Doc looked at the young girl as he turned her hand, applying the gel and wrapping the fingers.

"That was pretty brave of you," he whispered. She only stared at him.

"Who are you?" she asked.

"We're an organization that helps girls just like you. We rescue them." The suspicious stare continued, and he felt her gaze boring into him. "We were all former military. We have training, and this is what we choose to do with our lives now. I was a medic, but I'm also a PA."

"I..." she started to speak when Ghost sat on the other side of her. She flinched, and he smiled at her.

"This is my friend. We call him Ghost, but his real name is Eric. What's your name?" he asked casually.

"Terri."

"Nice to meet you, Terri," said Ghost. "We're going to get you all home soon, don't worry." She nodded and looked away from the other girls.

"It wasn't them," she said quietly. Ghost tilted his head, and Doc looked up at her, finishing the bandage on her hand.

"It wasn't them what, honey?" asked Doc.

"They... they didn't kill the old man. I did. I had to. It was the only way. Don't make them part of it. I made the decision to do it. I planned it out. It was me, not them." Ghost's eyes filled with tears, and he nodded at the girl.

"Let me tell you something, Terri," said Doc. "What you did was the bravest fucking thing I've ever seen in my life. You saved those girls, all of them. No one, and I mean no one, is going to blame you for that."

Her eyes filled with tears, and he reached out to touch her hand. She flinched slightly, but he just lay his big hand beside hers.

"I want you to promise me something, Terri. Promise me that when you get home, you'll find someone to talk to about all this, okay? You need to know that none of this was your fault. None of it."

"But it was," she said, the tears falling more freely now. Hawk watched the girl, and his heart cracked with her pain. "I went to that stupid party. I liked that boy that asked me to go. I danced..."

"I did too," said another girl. "All of us, the three of us were asked to the party together. We shouldn't have gone." Ghost nodded his head at the girls.

"Listen to me, all of you. You're right. You shouldn't have gone."

"Ghost..." said Bree, stepping forward. He held up his hand.

"You shouldn't have gone, but none of this is your fault. People go to parties they shouldn't go to all the time. They go to places they shouldn't go to all the time. Now you know. Now you'll never go to another party again without knowing exactly who, what, when and where. But know this, Terri, all of you, I've spent my life in the military around heroes, and I have never seen such fine heroes in all my life as what I'm looking at right now at this table."

The girls smiled at the big hairy man and went back to their sandwiches. Tango walked in the door with four women following him.

"Social services are here." The first woman looked at the table and swallowed.

"Oh my God," she whispered. Bree walked up to the women and introduced herself, filling them in on as much as she knew. She then introduced the girls to the four women, and they loaded up in the vans.

"Hawk? Eagle?" said Ghost. "Follow the vans and make sure those kids get to the hospital and then that their parents, and only their parents, take them out of there." The men nodded as Doc and Ghost stepped out onto the porch. The door to the van opened, and Terri stepped out, walking toward them again. She hugged Doc, thanking him for bandaging her hands and feet, then hugged Ghost.

"That lady in there said she's having your baby," she said. Ghost nodded, grinning at the girl. "You're going to be a great dad." He hugged the girl once more, and as they pulled out of the driveway, tears fell down his cheeks. Doc gripped his shoulders, and they held one another in a manly hug for a few moments.

"Hardest fucking thing ever," said Doc. Inside, the girls thanked the older woman for her kindness and then headed home with the guys.

It was done. The girls were safe and headed home.

"It's not done yet," said Doc as if reading their thoughts. "We still have to find Mabel and Anton."

"We're going to hunt them down," said Ghost. "When we're done, they'll know exactly who we are."

CHAPTER FORTY-SEVEN

Bree was sound asleep by the time they pulled into the cottage. Doc lifted her from the truck and opened the door, laying her on the bed before returning to lock the door. What a long fucking few weeks. He had to focus on the fact that they'd brought the girls home. They would be safe and in their parents' care by tomorrow.

Hopefully, as Terri so wisely stated, none of them would ever take an invitation to a party again without knowing more information. He wished he could record the whole thing and use it for PSAs with schools, but he knew that for whatever reason, many parents didn't want to discuss such things with their children.

Stripping off his clothes, he turned on the shower and stepped into the hot spray. The smell of the girls clung to his clothing and skin, needing to wash it away was a priority for his mental health right now. He heard Bree moan and smiled, knowing that she would most likely want to shower as well.

He left the water running and stepped out, wrapping a towel around his waist and another rubbing his hair and beard.

"Shower's hot, baby..." he stopped mid-sentence. Bree was seated on the edge of the bed, Mabel standing next to her with a pistol pointed at her head.

"You have ruined my fucking life," she spat. "My entire fucking life was wrapped up in this last shipment of girls. All of it. You've ruined it."

"You don't want, Bree. You want me. I rescued those girls. Me. Let her go," he pleaded.

"Are you kidding me right now? I know who you are now." Doc stood straighter, staring at the woman. "That's right. I know. That fuck-wad Anton knew and didn't tell me until it was too late. I should have put a bullet in your brain at Niagara."

"Mabel, please don't do this," pleaded Bree. She shoved the end of the pistol against her temple, Bree wincing in pain.

"Shut up! One shipment. One last shipment, and none of you would have ever known. I would have left the country. Well, now I'll leave the country, but I'm going to leave knowing you two are wiped from this planet." Doc looked down at Bree's beautiful face, her hands tucked beneath her legs, her palms flat on the bed.

"Don't do this, Mabel. They'll hunt you down. You know they will. You kill us, and you'll never get out of the country. You won't have Anton's help this time, and my team will hunt you down. Leave now. I won't come after you."

"You mean for now?" she said, laughing. "Do you think I'm such an idiot? I know you'll come for me sooner or later, and I can't have that!"

Bree let her hand lift slightly, and he saw it. Her cell phone was connected to someone, the timing showing it had been running for the last six minutes. Six minutes was how long it would take them at top speed to get from the club to her house.

"The girls are safe, you know," said Doc. "They didn't know who took them. You could leave, and they wouldn't be able to identify you."

"Jesus, you just don't get it, do you? I could give a shit anymore about the girls. You two are going to pay for all the misery you've caused me in the last few weeks. Sit beside her," she said, waving the gun in his direction.

That's when Doc saw it, the swirling red laser light of a scoped rifle through the window. The front door crashed open, and Mabel was distracted just long enough for him to dive on top of Bree. Three rapid rounds fired through the bedroom window, and he felt the sprays of hot liquid on his back.

"Fuck! Don't tell me I'm shot again?" he said against Bree's head.

"Wh-what? No, no, it's her blood. It's Mabel's." Doc stood, and standing behind him were Whiskey and Tango. Coming in the backdoor was Skull and Razor.

"You boys took long enough," said Bree, grinning at them. She was surprisingly calm, and Doc looked at her a bit worried. "I'm fine. Shaky, but fine. She needed to die, and if I'm being honest, I needed to see it. While you were in the shower, she said she'd been planning to take the last of this money and head to the Caribbean. She was sick, truly sick."

Doc nodded, pulling her against his bare chest. Once again, they had to wait for the sheriff and a coroner. It was nearly four a.m. by the time the house was locked, the door fixed, and the windows boarded.

"I don't think I want to live here anymore," said Bree.

"Then we won't, baby. We'll live at the club until my townhouse is done, and then we'll live there." She nodded.

"Will you just hold me tonight?"

"Forever, baby. Forever."

EPILOGUE

Bree and Grace were busy decorating the club for Christmas, lights hanging everywhere, stockings on the walls, the scents of orange and cinnamon filling the air, and even Christmas music playing. The fifteen-foot spruce was standing in the corner, the smell of its needles mixing with the cinnamon and orange.

Grace and Ghost made a quick decision to run off over the weekend and finally get married. Neither wanted a big wedding but wanted to be married before the birth of the baby. The team threw them a huge party upon their return, even delivering baby gifts along with the wedding presents for their new home.

It had been four days since Mabel was killed; since the girls were returned to their families and beginning their lives with a new awareness of the world, a new sense of normalcy that their young minds would need to adjust to.

"This place looks like the fucking north pole," said Whiskey, staring at the big open space of Club Steel.

"Oh, don't be such a scrooge," said Doc. "Grace and Bree both love Christmas, so let them have this. Besides, remember how great

Thanksgiving was? Holidays with the women around seem to be getting better and better, and I, for one, appreciate it. We've never had this, all of this. Being overseas all those years, and then it just being us here for so long. It's kinda nice having a woman's touch to the holidays." Whiskey only nodded, a cynical look on his face. Ace walked through the front door, a scowl on his face, his shirt stretched tight across his muscled chest. He stood at the table and slammed down a small bag.

"I told you all there were two things that needed to be done," he said, staring at Ghost and Doc. "You all did what you needed to do. You went after those girls. I did what I needed to do. What Bree needed. I went after Carl."

Doc opened the bag seeing a few items he didn't recognize. There was an old pocket watch, a ring, a little girl's diary, and a small blue vase. He raised an eyebrow at Ace.

"It's done. Carl doesn't exist anymore. I told y'all one of us needed to go. Took it upon myself to finish that asshole. He was still in the same apartment. Her room still looked exactly the same. That's where I got those things. Mother died almost four years ago. It's done." Doc nodded, smiling at his friend.

"Any word from Ivan?" asked Ghost.

"Nothing. I'm really worried about him. He usually checks in with me every few days," said Whiskey. "If I don't hear anything in the next few days, I may have our contact at the bureau start looking for him." Ghost and Doc nodded as the front door to the club opened.

Entering through the doors was a woman they all recognized. She was tall, blonde, blue-eyed, and currently very dirty with a black eye and split lip. She had a slight limp as she moved toward the man her eyes were locked onto.

"Fuck! Katarina!" said Whiskey, running to the young woman. "Are you okay?" She shook her head, shaking from the cold. She had on the same white sweater he'd seen her in that day at the library and only a thin jacket over that. Her hands were red and raw, her cheeks chapped and flushed from the wind.

"It... It took me a while to find you," she said, shaking. "I-I asked around and finally hitched a ride up here. The p-people in town pointed me this way."

"Honey, come in. What happened?" he asked, seating her at their table. Bree and Grace rushed to her side, grabbing a blanket and wrapping it around her shoulders. Bree set a glass of water in front of her, and Grace rushed to pour a cup of coffee. He could already hear her directing the kitchen to bring out hot food.

"My father, he sent his men to bring me to the house. I didn't have a choice. They pulled me from my home and shoved me into the car. When I got there, Omar was there."

"Fucking hell," said Whiskey.

"H-he sold me. He sold me to that man for a million dollars," she sniffed. "My own father... my own father sold me to that man. He said it was time to pay my debt. I refused, tried to run, I kicked my father, and he punched me. Omar tried to grab my arm, and when I shoved him, he slapped me across the face and hit me again. When I stood... I just ran. I've been running for five days. I tried to get some things from my house, but they're watching it. I... you didn't give me a card... I couldn't call you."

"It's okay, honey. You came to the right place," said Bree.

"What do you need me to do," asked Whiskey. "Just tell me. Anything." She swallowed, taking a sip of the whiskey sitting in front of her.

"I need you to kill my father and Omar Khanaman."

OTHER BOOKS BY MARY KENNEDY YOU

MIGHT ENJOY!

REAPER Security Series
Erin's' Hero
Lauren's Warrior
Lena's' Mountain
Sara's' Chance
Mary's Angel
Kari's Gargoyle
Rachelle's Savior
Adele's Heart
Tori's' Secret
Finding Lily
Montana Rules
Savannah Rain
Gray Skies
My First Choice
Three Wishes
Second Chances
One Day at a Time
When You Least Expect It
Missing Hearts
Trail of Love

My SEAL Boys (connections to the REAPER Series)
Ian
Noa
Carter
Lars
Trevor
Fitz
Chris
O'Hara

Strange Gifts Series
Dark Visions
Dark Medicine
Dark Flame

Steel Patriots MC Series
Ghost – Book One

ABOUT THE AUTHOR

Mary Kennedy is the mother of two adult children, has an amazing son-in-law, and is grandmother to two beautiful grandsons. She works full-time at a job she loves, and writing is her creative outlet. She lives in Texas and enjoys traveling, reading, and cooking. Her passion for assisting veterans and veteran causes comes from a strong military family background. Mary loves to hear from her readers and encourages them to join her mailing list, as she'll keep you up-to-date on new releases at https://insatiableink.squarespace.com. You can also join her Facebook page at Insatiable Ink.

Dear Readers,

I love hearing from you and encourage you to visit my website Insatiable Ink. Leave me know your thoughts and ideas on new books or expanding on characters. It's also a safe space to give your own feelings, like those of the characters. I love reading about how you relate to the stories because as we all know, there's a little of each of them within us.

I look forward to hearing from you and hope you enjoy other books in my collections.

Explore... and enjoy!